DEADHEAD

Bedhead Book Three

KAYT MILLER

Editor: Hot Tree Editing

Proofreading by: Hot Tree Editing

Formatted by: Kayt Miller

❀ Created with Vellum

CONTENTS

ALSO BY KAYT MILLER

For more information: www.kaytmiller.com

Bedhead

Redhead

Deadhead

FarmBoy

Game Changer

One of a Kind

The Virginia Chronicles

Our of the Blue: The Flynns Book One

Mick'sology: The Flynns Book Two

Vested Interest: The Flynns Book Three

The Importance of Being Ernie: The Flynns Book Four

The Importance of Being Kennedy's: The Flynns Book Five

Quirky Girl: The Flynns Book Six

The Art of the Game

Lainie: The Palmer Sisters Book 1

Agatha: The Palmer Sisters Book 2

Sadie: The Palmer Sisters Book 3

Cortland: The Palmer Sisters Book 4

Keely: The Palmer Sisters Book 5

Violet: The Palmer Sisters Book 6

Molly: The Palmer Sisters Book 7

The Portrait Painter

Hopeful Romantic (Coming soon.)

Thanks to Margie Dill (Coming soon.)

PROLOGUE

Gage

I don't remember a time when I didn't want to be a cop. When I was little, my brother and I would play that game Cops and Robbers, and I was *always* the cop while my brother Graham was always the robber. Funny how life works out. Now Graham is *always* in some kind of trouble, and I'm always bailing him out. Literally and figuratively. Luckily, he lives in Missouri, so I don't have to witness any of it firsthand, or worse, arrest him.

But there are days, like today, that I wish I did something else. *Anything* else. Hell, re-upping in the army sounds pretty damn appealing after the shit that went down today. That's because today I have to arrest a friend. Well, a friend of a friend, I guess you'd say. No, she's a friend. Believe me, I tried to get out of it. I told the captain I knew the suspect personally, but he didn't bat an eye. Instead of understanding, he snapped, "You're the senior uniform on duty, Golden. Get out there and do your goddamn job."

So one of the rookies and I take off, heading to Tayler and Quinn's place, with me hoping like hell Quinn won't be around for this. The second the door swings open and Tayler Sorenson smiles at me, my stomach flips. Then again when she uses her nicest voice and says, "Oh hi, Gage. What's up?"

Then once more when Luke Green appears behind her. "Hey, man."

For a second I forget why I'm here. I'm supposed to be in cop mode, but that left me on the ride over, I guess. "Uh, hey." Yeah, I sound like an idiot. As quickly as I can, I clear my throat and do what I came to do. "Tayler Sorenson?"

She's still smiling at me. *God, this sucks.* "Yes."

"I need to ask you to come with us."

She laughs. She thinks this is a joke. Man, I wish it were. "Why?" she asks, tilting her head just a little bit. I'd say it's adorable if any of this was fun.

Apparently the rookie officer, Lance Finch, has had enough of my hemming and hawing. "Tayler Sorenson, we'd like you to come with us. If you come with us willingly, we won't cuff you."

I want to cuff *him*, the jackass. That was unnecessary. I told him in the fucking squad car that I'd handle this–, that I knew Tayler personally, but this guy just has to play bad cop whenever he gets the chance. The guy drives me nuts.

"Cuff her? What the fuck, Gage?" Luke snaps. "What's going on?"

I get why he's pissed. Hell, I'm angry about this too, but I've got a job to do, and I'm not about to let Finch take the lead on this. Looking at Tayler, I say, "Tayler, where were you last night between the hours of ten and midnight?"

"Here."

Okay. That's good. She was home. This is going to be a piece of cake. Please, for the love of God, don't tell me you were alone.

I look at Luke. "Were you here as well, Mr. Green?"

"No. I was at work."

Not the answer I wanted, so I shake my head because damn it. "You were alone, Ms. Sorenson?"

"Yes. I was alone until Luke got home." She looks at Finch, then at me. "What's going on?"

"Tayler Sorenson," Finch starts up again, "you're under arrest for the murder of Kara Becker."

I want to punch this asshole.

"Murder?" Luke and Tayler say at the same time. "Under arrest?"

I want to give her some advice. If I could, I'd say things like "Don't say a word" or "Just come with us now and get a good lawyer," but I can't. Luckily, Luke says everything I'd say if she were mine. Which she isn't. Neither is her best friend, Quinn. Sadly.

"Tayler," Luke says to her, "I'll call my lawyer. Just go with them. But, babe?" He sounds like he knows what he's doing. "Say. Nothing."

"But I didn't do anything." Her voice is a little whiny, but I get it. Mine would be too, probably. Besides, suspects always say that, but I want to believe she's telling the truth. I really do.

Luke repeats, "I know, but promise me you'll wait for the attorney. I'll be right behind you. Don't worry, Tayler."

I watch as Tayler reaches to her right to retrieve something. When she steps back in front of the opening, she's got her purse. She's still in sleepwear, but she's not wearing shoes.

"Tayler, if you'd like to get dressed." I look down at her feet. "And put on some shoes. We'll wait." Strange. It's the second time in the last eight hours I've asked a woman to get dressed.

Finch makes a grunting noise, but I don't even look his way. I'm so pissed at him that I won't bother acknowledging him now. I'll deal with *him* later.

CHAPTER ONE

Gage

H*ours earlier.*

"NEAREST AVAILABLE UNIT. 10-83 1320 COCONINO ROAD. Apartment 2-1-3."

I'm in west Ames, so knowing I'm likely the closest, I press my radio button and respond as I hit the gas on my cruiser. "10-4 dispatch. 1320 Concocino Road. Rolling up."

Finally I've got something to do. I've driven around for the last three hours hoping for something to happen. No, I'm not hoping for something *terrible* to happen, just something— *anything*. I'll even take this 10-83 —a welfare check. Something we do a lot of in this town. It happens when parents call us to check on their college kids because they won't answer their phones or reply to text messages. I guess these kids are too busy. Either that or they're afraid to talk to their folks. I'd figure the latter to be the case more often than not.

This welfare check is going to be something similar, because 1320 Coconino Road is an apartment complex designed for student living. I looked at that place when I first moved to Ames four years ago. It was brand new then, and while it had a ton of cool amenities, like several pools, a 24-7 fitness center, a dog park, and a social club, I couldn't picture myself living among a bunch of college students partying all the time. And would they want a cop living above them? Doubtful.

No, at that time, I'd just left the army, and all I wanted was a quiet place to call home. It's why I bought my small house instead of renting. That and I was ready to put down some roots some-where. I moved all over the place for four years as a military police officer, or MP, and I didn't want to do that any longer. Now that I've been in this job for four years, I still feel that way most of the time. However, lately I've started to get a bit antsy, like I'm ready for the next phase of my life. I want whatever's supposed to come next.

Pulling into the parking lot of the Social Apartment complex, I park. Grabbing my notebook and pen, I jot down the time—2:37 a.m.—then slide it into my breast pocket. A strange time for a welfare check. Whoever called it in may have tried to reach this resident for a while and just gave up. It happens.

Outside my squad car, I scan the perimeter. It's the middle of the night, so the lights they've got on the parking lot are enough to allow me to see a good distance. Walking past one building, I note the address number. Looking for the one with 1320 on the sign, I see it ahead.

Opening the main door, I step into a spacious area with couches and tables. It's still pretty nice considering the people who live here. College students can be hard on a place, another reason for me to buy my own. I found a fixer-upper that was dirt cheap. Over the last few years, I've almost redone the whole place. All I have left to do is finish the basement and rebuild the garage. The garage isn't in terrible shape, but I'd like to use it as a workshop, and there's just not enough room in my current one-car structure.

Taking the steps two-at-a-time, I'm up on the second floor in no time, searching for apartment 213.

Strange. I know this apartment. I've been here before.

Raising my hand, I knock lightly at first. Waiting a few seconds, I knock again. "Police," I say in my normal voice. "Welfare check." When I get no response, I press the button next to the door and hear the chime. Still nothing. Whoever lives here is either asleep or gone, but I'm going to have to enter the place to be sure. Hearing a squeak behind me, I quickly turn and scan the hallway, expecting to see someone leaving their apartment. It's the middle of the night, but there's no such thing for some of these college kids.

I ring the bell again and wait. When I hear nothing from inside, I reach for the knob and turn and am shocked to feel it give. Who leaves their door unlocked these days? Nobody should, that's for sure. No matter how safe your neighborhood is, lock your damn door.

When it unlatches, I slowly push the door open and repeat, "Police." I take one step over the threshold, then another into a short hallway. To my right is a small kitchen. I peer inside and see dirty dishes in the sink and what looks like a pan on the stove that's burned dry. I move closer and see not only burnt, hardened pasta inside, but the burner is still on. "Not good," I mutter to myself. Lucky the place didn't burn down. Reaching out, I turn off the stove.

Back in the short hallway, I repeat, "Police. Welfare check." Walking slowly, I enter a smallish living space. There's a sofa, chair, television stand, and a small dining table with two chairs. The furniture looks nice. Top of the line. I know because I just replaced my living room furniture, and that shit's expensive. Yeah, the stuff in this place is way too nice for a student apartment.

When I note the room is clear, I approach a mostly closed door. Looks to be a bedroom. Reaching up, I knock. "Police." Again, no response.

Since the door isn't shut all the way, I reach up toward the top and push it open, then freeze for a moment. She's there. I rush to the form on the floor. The one facedown with blood pooled around her head. Reaching out, I place my fingers on her neck to feel for a pulse. Nothing.

I knew it. I've seen bodies before in the service and one other time here in Ames. There are tells like the odor, the deep reddish brown color of the blood on the floor, the body temperature. She's cold, but rigor hasn't set in yet and the odor isn't overwhelming. Not yet.

Reaching for the radio on my shoulder, I press the button. "10-35, 10-78. 1320 Coconino Road, number 2-1-3. Officer needs assistance."

"10-4. 11-44. 1320 Coconino Road, number 2-1-3. Units responding."

As soon as the call is in, I stand and back out of the bedroom, making sure I don't touch anything else. My hand has been on the top of the bedroom door, the front doorknob, and the stove. I'll have to report that as soon as the others get here.

Stepping out into the hallway, I turn so I'm facing the door across the hall. This is where I'll wait for the homicide team, which will include the coroner, the detective on duty, and several uniformed officers. We'll need to knock on all these doors soon so we can start asking questions. The more people we have on hand, the faster that will go.

It's then that I see movement to my right, followed by the sound of a click—like someone just shut their door. The source of the sound is across the hallway and one over. Walking to that door, I raise my hand and knock. The sound I heard earlier, before I entered the deceased's apartment, came from this location too. Whoever lives in this place has been watching me. "Police. May I speak to you?"

When there's no response, I knock again. "Police. Open up."

I hear the clicking sound again and realize it's the deadbolt sliding open. Staring down at the knob, I watch it turn slowly. I'm about to knock again because I'm getting impatient when the door begins to open. Begins is the right word for it, because that's all it does. The thing is open between a quarter to half an inch. My line of sight follows the opening until it meets one eye. One eye that's peeking out the sliver of an opening.

"Yes?" the voice says so softly it's barely audible. But it's enough for me to tell the voice is female. Good thing because I can't tell from the eyeball peering back at me.

I point to the badge on my chest. "Officer Golden. Ames PD. What's your name?"

There's a long pause. Is she trying to figure out what her name is?

"D-Daisy."

"Daisy? Daisy, what's your last name?"

"B-Buchanan."

I reach into my front pocket and retrieve my small notebook and pen, quickly jotting down the name.

"Daisy Buchanan? Can I speak to you for a moment?" The eyeball moves up and down. I'm going to take that as a yes. "Would you mind opening up the door?"

The eyeball moves up and down again.

Okay. I guess she doesn't want to open the door.

"I'm not dressed." Her voice is now above a whisper but only slightly.

"Can you get dressed so I can speak with you? It's urgent."

"I-Is she okay?" The eyeball looks to my left. Toward the open door of the apartment with the deceased.

"I'm not at liberty to say at this time. Can you please get dressed so we can ask you some questions?"

"We?" she squeaks. Why does she sound terrified?

"Yes. We. There'll be more police here soon."

"Wh-What?" she says, sounding terrified. "Why?"

"If you'll get dressed, I'll be able to tell you more after you answer a few questions." Which isn't entirely true. I can't tell her anything other than her neighbor is dead. She'll have to find out everything else the same as the rest of the world—in the news.

Without another word, she shuts the door, and I hear the latch click back into place.

Great. Hopefully the detective will have better luck when he gets here.

CHAPTER TWO

Gage

"What the hell's going on, Gage? Tayler didn't *kill* anyone. She can barely kill a spider."

I knew this was coming. Well, I expected a visit from Quinn Maxwell, at least, since Tayler's her best friend, but she's still in England, apparently. *With the boyfriend.* In her stead, the rest of the women who lived with her on Beedle Drive have cornered me outside of the Ames police station just as I was heading home for the night. Now I've got to deal with the rest of her tight-knit group of friends.

Right now, it's Patsy.

"Patsy." I place my hands on my hips. "I can't talk about an open case."

"This is fucking ridiculous." Robbi, short for Roberta, is the outspoken one and sort of intimidating, if I'm being honest. "Quinn's so upset she's about ready to jump on a plane even though Cooke's still recuperating."

I'd like to see Quinn, but not under these circumstances. "This can't be helped."

"Sure it can," says Susanna, Patsy's sister, from the back of the group. "Just let her go. This is crazy."

"She'll be arraigned. After that, I'm sure she'll be able to post bail." I don't know why I said that. I'm not sure about anything.

"Arraigned?" Lindsay squeaks. "Bail?"

"How's Luke handling all of this?" Robbi's got her arms crossed in front of her, and her hip is jutted to the right. Yeah, she's angry.

"I couldn't say." Because while I've seen him, I haven't spoken to him. Tayler's attorney showed up and told her not to speak. Then she was placed in a cell, and that was that.

"How *is* Tayler?" Patsy's sounding a bit forlorn.

"She's holding up." I checked on her right before I changed out of my uniform. She'd been crying, but she seemed to be okay. "You all just need to head home and let this process play out."

"This 'process'"—Robbi uses air quotes—"is bullshit."

"Uh-huh." I start to walk away from the group because the direction Robbi's heading isn't going to help anyone.

"Just tell us why you think she did it." I'm not sure which woman asks the question. My guess would be Patsy.

Turning back around, I see the worry on all their young faces. "I'm not at liberty to say much, but I can say there was an eyewitness."

One by one, their expressions change from worry to something completely different.

"Bullshit." Robbi again.

"Ladies, that's all I can say for now. The detective in charge of the case is Dan Trumbull."

"But you're going to help, right, Gage?" Katherine Kramer, better known as Kat, steps forward. "Quinn would want you to help find the *real* killer."

These Beedle Babes, as Quinn calls them, have all got the impression that Quinn and I have some sort of special friendship. We don't. Sure, my heart sort of did a little flip-flop when I first met Quinn, but that lasted until the day I met *the boyfriend*. She's got someone in her life, and she seems happy. That's all there is to it. Still, I care about Quinn. I probably always will. She's unique. Special. Beautiful. I've got more adjectives I could use to describe her, but why bother? That ship has sailed. I missed my chance with her. Period.

"I'm assisting on the case." At least according to my captain, and much to my chagrin. Like I said, I'm too close to this one.

"So you'll find the *real* killer," Kat states, again, like it's a done deal.

It's not.

I blink at the women, wondering what I need to say to get them out of here. I'm tired and so damn hungry having worked a double shift thanks to the murder of Kara Becker.

With a sigh, I place my hands on my hips. I might as well take advantage of the fact they're all there. Hell, if Quinn were here in the States, I'm afraid she'd be sitting in the station for questioning as well. I may as well ask them a few. "Let me ask you all something. When was the last time you each saw Kara Becker?"

There's a backstory here that needs to be addressed. These women—Patsy and Susanna, in particular—have known Kara for years. Their mom works for her father. Kara was supposed to live with this group of women in their rental on Beedle Drive here in Ames. Instead, Quinn moved in, which infuriated Kara. The two were at odds for a while. So much so that Kara destroyed Quinn's scooter and was undeniably out to get Quinn. All of it forced Kara's father to drag her out of Ames, promising everyone that she'd transfer to another school. Apparently, that didn't happen.

"When did *we* see Kara last?" asks Lindsay.

I nod. "When was the last time each of you saw Kara?"

"I haven't seen her since she moved back home," Lindsay answers first.

"We"—Patsy points to her little sister—"saw her when we went home the last time."

"When was that?" I reach up to grab my notebook, but I'm not wearing my uniform, only my old army tee. Pulling out my phone, I open my Notes application, then look up at Patsy, waiting for her response.

"March?" she asks, looking at her sister.

"Yeah, spring break," Susanna replies.

"Right," Patsy says, nodding.

"I'll come back to that." I say to the sisters. Turning to Robbi, I ask. "What about you, Robbi? Did you know Kara Becker was back in town?"

Surprisingly, Robbi's quiet. But only for a second. "I saw her. At Cy's."

I can't help noticing the looks on the other women's faces. They're obviously surprised to hear that Robbi had seen her in town.

I look down at my phone and type, asking, "When?"

"Last weekend."

"Who was she with?"

"Uh, I'm not sure. I was sitting at the bar with Bull. She stepped up, saw me, then turned and left. It was weird."

"So you didn't see her in the bar prior to that?"

Robbi shakes her head. "No."

"Have you seen her since?"

I get another head shake.

"Did you happen to mention to anyone else that you'd seen Kara?"

When Robbi doesn't answer my question, I look up from my notes. "Robbi? Did you hear my question?"

She nods slowly.

"And?"

I've been a cop long enough to know that silence can be deafening. "You know you're going to be officially questioned, right? You need to be prepared to answer questions truthfully." I arch my brow and look directly at Robbi.

"Um... I sent Tayler a text."

I'm not sure who, but someone gasps.

Glaring at her friends, then at me, she snaps, "I did it so she'd warn Quinn." Robbi's voice rises, sounding defensive.

Patsy reaches out and places her hand on Robbi's shoulder. "We would have done the same thing, Rob."

"Why will *we* be questioned?" Lindsay asks with a squeaky voice.

"Because you knew the victim and you know the accused," I explain.

"This is all such bullshit," Robbi spits. "Tayler wouldn't hurt a fly."

I know Tayler's a nice woman and all, and she may not hurt a fly, but she might just hurt the person who was out to get her best friend. She's not as sweet and innocent as people are making her out to be. I witnessed it firsthand sitting in her living room. She threatened Kara's life that day when I told her and Quinn that Kara was moving back to Ames. Actually, she said something like *"Kara had better hope she never crosses my path. I'll fucking kill her."*

So there's that.

"Thanks for agreeing to talk to me here."

The next afternoon, Finch and I are sitting in the living room of the house on Beedle Drive. I warned him to keep his mouth shut this time. He agreed. Each of Quinn's former roommates are present, including Lindsay, Patsy, Susanna, Robbi, and Kat. A guy known as Bull, real name Brandon Kemp, is also here since he was with Robbi the night she saw Kara at Cy's Roost.

"Ask us anything you want, Gage," Patsy says, smiling. "Whatever we need to do to help Tayler, we'll do it."

I nod, scanning the small group. "So, Robbi, you saw Kara Becker at Cy's Roost."

Robbi nods.

"Bull? Do you remember seeing her as well?"

"I didn't know who she was, but Robbi mentioned something to me after she left."

"What did she say?"

Bull looks over at Robbi, who nods. Looking back at me, he says, "She said she was the bitch who was harassing Quinn."

"What was your response to that?"

He looks at Robbi again. Same thing. She nods, and then he answers, "I asked her if she wanted me to...." He hesitates, looking at Robbi again. She nods. "I, uh, asked her if she wanted me to handle that."

"Handle that?" Shit. Is this guy incriminating himself? "What did you mean by that?"

"You know. Talk to her."

"Talk?"

"Yeah. Talk." He grunts, his expression stormy. "I'd *never* hurt a girl."

"Of course not, babe," Robbi says, patting his hand. "We all know you're a teddy bear under all that muscle."

Bull smiles down at Robbi, but when he looks at me, he glares as he continues, "Robbi said no, and I never saw her after that night."

"Robbi?" I look at her. "You never saw Kara after that initial sighting at Cy's?"

"No."

"You didn't go to her apartment?"

"No. I wasn't sure where she lived." She shrugs.

"A simple search online would have given you that information." I know because I tried it.

"I didn't visit her. Why would I?"

Ignoring her question, I decide to change directions a little. "When did you contact Tayler about seeing Kara?"

"That night. I sent her a text."

"Is that message still on your phone?"

Robbi nods.

"May I see the exchange?"

With a curse I can't quite make out, Robbi reaches behind her, retrieving her phone. "I know I should make you get a warrant or something, but if this helps Tayler...."

I can't address that comment until I've seen the messages.

Robbi clicks around on her phone until she finds what I need. She hands it to me, and I begin to read as Finch leans in to read over my shoulder.

I hate that.

Robbi: Yo. I just spotted that bitch Kara at Cy's.

It looks as though Tayler replied right away.

Tayler: What the hell? Seriously?
Robbi: Seriously.
Tayler: Is she still there?
Robbi: No. She saw me and left.
Tayler: I thought her father promised he'd keep her out of Ames.
Robbi: No clue. Do you want me to do anything?
Tayler: No. I'll take care of it.
Robbi: You sure?
Tayler: Positive. I'm just glad Quinn's not here. Who knows what that psycho would do?
Robbi: Word.
Tayler: LOL. Word?
Robbi: Bringing back a classic.
Tayler: How's Bull? <3
Robbi: Bull... Bull is a surprise.
Tayler: What does that mean? Are you talking sexually, because I don't need to know. LOL
Robbi: It means Bull is nothing like I thought he was. And yes, sexually he's got a BIG surprise.

Tayler. NO! TMI!

Robbi: LOL. Sorry. Not sorry.

Tayler: Well, thanks for letting me know. Not about Bull!!!

Robbi: Ha! No problem.

The only part of this exchange that sounds a bit dubious is when Tayler says, "I'll take care of it." Otherwise, there wasn't anything out of the ordinary. Well, except I didn't need to know about Bull and his....

Looking up at Robbi, I ask her if she'd send me a copy of this exchange. When she agrees, I hand back her phone, saying, "This may need to be taken into evidence."

"Whatever," she grumbles.

Turning back to Patsy and Susanna, I say, "Tell me more about your interaction with Kara while you were home."

The two sisters look at each other, and then Patsy speaks. "We ran into her at the convenience store in our hometown."

"When was that again?" I ask, jotting down that information.

"Like, um, March 18?" Susanna's response sounds like more of a question. She looks at her sister. "Right?"

"Around there." Patsy nods. "I remember it was dinnertime because we were picking up pizza."

"Was Kara alone?" I ask.

"I think so." Patsy looks at Susanna, who nods.

"Can you remember who spoke first?"

"I did," says Susanna. "I said hello and asked her how she was doing."

"What did she say?"

"She smiled." Susanna shakes her head. "No. It was more than that. She was beaming."

"She was." Patsy nods. "But Kara could put on an act if needed."

Shaking her head, Susanna disputes Patsy's theory. "No. She

was really happy. She said she had a lot going on and that she had big plans. I figured she meant going to the University of Iowa or something, but our pizza was ready then, so I didn't get a chance to ask her."

I look up after writing my notes. "Did she say anything else?"

The two women look at each other, then back at me. "I don't remember," Patsy answers.

With a nod, Susanna has something, "She said she'd see us around."

"Did you think she meant she'd see you in Ames?" I ask.

Shrugging, Susanna shakes her head. "No. I thought she meant around town, you know, in Stuart."

I turn to Kat and Lindsay. "Neither of you saw Kara in Ames prior to her death?"

Both women shake their heads.

I expected that response. Scanning the group again, I hope to get a little more. "Can you all think of people Kara spent time with when she was in Ames prior to or around the time she had issues with Quinn?"

The room is quiet until Kat raises her hand like we're in class.

"Yes?" I acknowledge her.

"She hung out with that guy Quinn liked." Leaning forward, she looks at the rest of the women in the room. "Right?"

"Yeah," Lindsay responds. "Quinn was sort of upset about that."

Kat nods. "She was."

"What was his name?" I ask.

Kat throws out, "It was something like Bradley." She turns to the group. "Right, guys?"

"I thought it was something like Braxton," Robbi adds.

I sigh inwardly. "Well, do you think you could find out for sure and call me?"

They all nod in unison. Well, not Bull. He's sitting next to Robbi as stiff as a board.

"Can you think of anyone else?"

Again, in unison, they all shake their heads. Even Bull joins in this time.

Shutting my notebook, I stand. "Robbi and Bull, you two may need to come down to the station to talk to the rest of the team."

"Sure." It's Bull who speaks for the pair.

Reaching into my breast pocket, I retrieve several of my cards. Placing them on the coffee table, I ask them to call me if they think of anything.

"We will." Patsy says, smiling. "We want to help Tayler any way we can."

"Thanks." I make my way to the front door. Reaching for the knob, I turn and repeat, "Seriously. *Any* information you think of, let me know. You'd be surprised what can help."

"We will," Patsy responds like she's the spokesperson for the group.

I suppose she is.

CHAPTER THREE

Gage

Strange. None of the women from Beedle Drive asked any questions about Kara. I know she wasn't a nice woman, but they hung out with her, yet none of them even asked how she died.

Pulling into my small two-bedroom bungalow, I put the car in Park and sit with it running. Come to think of it, neither Tayler *nor* Luke asked how she died. In my mind, if it were *me* being arrested, I think that'd be my first question. But I am a cop. Still, if they had, maybe knowing the cause and that it likely wasn't premeditated would help. Whoever killed her—and I'm not entirely convinced it was Tayler—grabbed the first thing they saw and *bam*. It's what we call a crime of passion. Which means anyone could have done it. The weapon of choice, a four iron from what appears to be Kara's golf bag, was something anyone could have grabbed and swung with enough force to kill a person. You don't have to be male or even especially strong to do the damage that was done, because the golf club did all the work.

Just then, I hear the phone vibrate in my pocket. Leaning back, I slide the phone out and see it's Quinn calling. I knew it was just a matter of time. I've been dreading this.

"Hello?" I answer with as much calm as I can muster.

"Oh my God, Gage. What's going on there? You arrested Tayler? For murder?" The last word came out as a loud sort of screech. "How could you? She'd never kill anyone. Trust me."

"Quinn—"

But she doesn't let me speak. "She'd never kill anyone. *Ever*. She's so happy. She and Luke finally figured their stuff out. She wouldn't jeopardize that."

"Quinn, listen—"

"You've got to find who really killed her, Gage."

"Quinn—"

"How'd she die, anyway?"

Finally! "Blunt force trauma."

"Huh?"

"She was hit over the head."

"Tayler couldn't hit anyone hard enough to kill them. She's a wimp. She's got no upper body strength."

I want to laugh. I really do. But this is serious.

"The weapon appears to have been a golf club." I shouldn't be saying anything to Quinn. They haven't released anything to the press. If it gets around that I'm telling people, especially the suspect's best friend, about the crime scene, I'd be reprimanded.

"Well, there you go. I know it wasn't her. Tayler *hates* golf."

That's it. I can't help it. I laugh. Which makes the other person on the phone grow silent. It's then I hear what sounds like sniffles. Quinn's crying.

Shit. "Quinn, I didn't mean to laugh."

More sniffles.

"Quinn?"

"She's my best friend, Gage. This is serious. She's in jail!" she wails. Between sobbing and deep breaths, she adds, "She didn't kill her. I know it. Can't you do something? Can't you investigate more? Because I promise you, Gage. Tayler. Didn't. Do it."

"It doesn't work like that. The detective in charge...." Is an asshole who thinks he's the best of the best, but the few times I've worked with him, I haven't been impressed.

"Please, Gage." Her voice sounds so sad and desperate. "I'm worried about her."

"Gage, mate." I can't help noticing Quinn's voice has gotten deeper and British.

I'd love to tell you that I liked Quinn's boyfriend, Cooke Thompson, famous rugby star, but that'd be a lie. I tolerate him for her sake. Don't get me wrong, he's a decent guy, but I had hopes for Quinn and me.

Shaking my head, I finally speak. "Hey, Cooke."

"Listen, mate, Quinn's bloody beside herself, and I can't do shite here to help her. We're getting on a flight day after tomorrow, but until then, can you please do whatever you can to find the real killer? You know she didn't do it, mate."

Mate? *We're not mates.*

"Please, Gage?" Quinn's voice comes back on the line, and it breaks my heart.

With a reluctant sigh, I say something I shouldn't. "I'll do some more digging. Okay?"

I can hear her blow her nose on the other end of the line, but then she says, "Thank you. Thank you so much, Gage. I know you'll find the real killer because you're the best police officer in Ames."

Okay, now she's just blowing smoke up my ass. "Right. I'll see you when you get back." Because she's not going to let this go. And I don't blame her.

"Bye, Gage."

"Bye, Quinn."

With a sigh, I put my car into Reverse, back out of my driveway, and head back over to Social Apartments. There's something our eyewitness said that's been bothering me. Might as well see if I can speak to Daisy Buchanan again. Maybe this time she'll open the door all the way.

~

THIS TIME WHEN I PULL INTO THE APARTMENT COMPLEX, I drive directly to 1320 and park. Reaching down to my left, I pop the trunk to retrieve my Ames PD wind jacket. Since I changed into street clothes at the station, I feel as though I need to wear something identifying me as a cop doing official business, plus it's getting colder now that fall's setting in. Pulling that over my head, I check my pocket for my badge and contemplate adding my holster but decide against it.

When I knock on Buchanan's door, I expect the same thing to happen as this morning, that she'll open it an inch and that's all, but surprisingly that's not the case. No, this time she opens it at least six inches. It's just enough to see her—well, most of her.

She's short. I knew that. I'd guess close to five-two or five-three. Her hair is dark, and from what I can gather from the size of the bun on top of her head, I'd say it's pretty long. She's wearing glasses now, which look too big for her smallish face. I suppose it helps to see the big eyes behind them. From here, I can't tell exactly what color her eyes are, but my best guess would be blue or perhaps gray. No matter the color, I feel a little taken aback by the size of them now that I can see two at once. Doe-eyed. That's a good word for her.

I quickly scan down her body and note her attire. An over-sized Iowa State sweatshirt hides her body and covers her down to her knees, where tights or leggings take over. Below that, I catch a flash of pink toenail polish on her bare feet.

"Officer Golden?"

"Oh, uh, yes." I clear my throat. "Miss Buchanan, would you mind if I asked you a few more questions?"

Her long lashes flutter behind her giant lenses. "More questions?" She sounds nervous.

"Yes. A few more."

Pushing the door open wider, she steps aside and gestures for me to enter. Which is weird because this morning, she wouldn't budge from her front door.

"Thanks," I say as I pass through her doorway to stand in what is a mirror image of Kara Becker's place. Daisy's kitchen is on my left, meaning her bedroom would be to the right after the small dining nook. "Nice place." I say it just to make small talk. Because it's not nice. I'd go so far as to call it a hoarder's paradise. She's got stuff everywhere. In the living area is a two-seater couch, but on either side of that are stacks of boxes and plastic containers that hold—I lean closer—magazines, maybe? Newspapers?

Not only that, there are boxes stacked up along the wall that should lead to a small deck space, but hers is completely blocked by brown cardboard. A small television, maybe a twenty-two-inch, rests on top of old milk crates that are filled with things. I can't tell what they are from here, but they look to be collectible items —tchotchkes is what my mom calls them.

"Yeah, well...." Clearing her throat, she points to the sofa. "Have a seat." She pulls up a tall stool that she takes from a spot near the kitchen. It's hard to tell for sure, because there's a rack that holds clothing that blocks that part of the apartment from this area.

"Thanks."

"Can I get you anything?" She's getting more nervous by the minute, but a small laugh seems to break the ice. "I've got water."

"No, thanks. I'm fine."

"Okay."

I watch her step on the rung of the stool to rise high enough to get into the seat. I changed my mind—if she's five feet tall, I'd be surprised.

"Did you just move in?" I'm not sure why I ask her that. I guess it's due to the stacked boxes against the wall. I point to them.

Shaking her head, she answers me. "No. This stuff was my mom's."

"Where's your mom?"

"Gone."

"Oh, I'm sorry for your loss."

I must have said something hilarious, because she throws her head back and laughs. Hard. Funny, I sort of like it. It's part giggle, part hearty laugh. "She's not *dead*. She's in—" She looks up for a moment. "—California now, I think."

"You're not sure?"

Daisy shrugs and, with a smile, tells me, "She sends postcards."

"What about your father?"

The smile drops from her face fast. "He's here."

I point downward. "Here? As in your apartment."

Rolling her eyes, Daisy shakes her head. "No. In Ames. He's a professor."

"At ISU?" Dumb question, but I have to ask.

"Yeah. American literature."

Taking my phone out of my back pocket, I open my Notes app and begin to type. "What's his name?"

"Why?" she snaps. "What do you need with *him*? And what are you typing?"

"Oh. Sorry." I place the phone down next to my leg. Chuckling, I reply, "Habit."

She releases a breath that makes me wonder what the deal is with Daisy and her father.

"His name is Dorian Buchanan." After a pause, she adds with an eye roll, "*Doctor* Dorian Buchanan."

"I take it you're not close to your dad."

She scoffs. "My father and I are definitely *not* close."

"Why's that?"

Sliding down from the stool, she crosses her arms in front of her. If I'm not careful, she's going to ask me to leave, and I've got more questions. "Does that really have anything to do with my neighbor? It sounds to me like you're digging for things that don't relate."

"Just curious."

She smirks. "Curiosity killed— the cat."

I hate that expression. It makes me think of my cat, Pepper Anderson, and I'd be really bummed if anything happened to her. I nod. "It did. But it's also my job."

Turning, she moves toward her kitchen. Looking back at me, she asks, "Sure you don't want some water?"

Maybe I should just accept. It could buy me some time. "Sure. I'll take some." I stand and follow her. I need to see her face as she responds to my queries. "So, did you know Kara Becker very well?"

"No. I thought she'd moved out until I saw her last week getting her mail."

"Did you speak with her?"

"I said hello to her, but that was it."

"Did she respond?"

Daisy shrugs. "She said hi back."

"So you didn't socialize with Ms. Becker?"

My question must surprise her because her head jerks up and our eyes meet. "Socialize?"

"Yeah. Did you hang out with her here?" I jerk my thumb toward the door. "At the pool or other facilities?"

"Um... no. I don't really socialize. With anyone."

"Why not? You're in school, aren't you?"

"No." She shakes her head. "I graduated two years ago."

"Oh? You look so young."

She chuckles. "Well, I'm not ancient. I'm twenty-three."

"I see."

"How old are you?" she asks, handing me a small glass or water with one ice cube.

"Twenty-seven."

"You look older."

Well, what do you say to that?' "Thanks?" I must have said the right thing because she laughs again. "*I'm* not ancient." I may as well play along.

"No." She chuckles. "You're not ancient either." She moves closer and stops. I'm not sure what she wants, so when she waves me off, I get it. I'm supposed to move out of the kitchen doorway so she can leave. I move to the side and let her pass. She's so close we almost touch. I can't help noticing how good she smells. It's sweet, pretty. Like her.

Okay. I don't know if she's sweet. Pretty, definitely. But from the two times I've interacted with her, sweet isn't a word I'd use to describe her. Leery is one. Tentative and shy, definitely.

"So, you didn't socialize with Kara. But you saw her now and then?" I ask.

"When she was here before, I'd see her down in the laundry room, in the lobby, that sort of thing. But we never said more than one or two words to each other."

"Did she have other friends from the complex?"

"Not that I know of. She had visitors, but I didn't make it a point to check out everyone who passed through her doorway."

"So, how do you know about the redhead?"

"I told you this already," she says, sounding irritated.

"One more time, please."

"Fine." She huffs. "I was coming up from the laundry room. The redhead was knocking on Kara's door."

"And what time was this?"

"Around ten."

"How can you be sure?"

"Because I set my timer on my phone to remind me to get my clothes out of the dryer. If you don't do that around here, people either dump your stuff on the floor or take it." She pauses. "Or both."

Picking up my phone, I search my photos for the mug shot of Tayler. Holding it out to her, I ask, "Is this the redhead?"

She nods. "I think so. I saw her from the back mostly but also in profile."

I turn my phone and bring up Tayler's photo in profile. "This her?"

"Yeah." She nods, looking solemn.

"Did you see anyone else approach Kara's door that night?"

"No."

"Did you hear anything? Any loud noises that night, between ten and midnight?"

"I put my headphones on as soon as I got back so I wouldn't hear anything."

That was a strange way to answer that question, but I won't read too much into it just yet. Though I am curious if she really meant *wouldn't* or rather *couldn't* hear anything?

"Can you think of anything else that can help us with our inquiry?" Daisy shakes her head, then does something surprising. She smiles. And it nearly takes my breath away. The woman's face lights up like a beacon. "You should smile more often," I say without thinking.

Wrong thing to say, because it goes away as quickly as it came.

Slipping off her stool again, she walks to her front door.

I guess it's time for me to go.

"I may have more questions for you," I warn her.

"Okay," she responds softly.

Reaching into my breast pocket, I retrieve my card. "My cell number is on the back. If you think of something or you're concerned about anything, give me a call."

"Concerned? About what?"

"Well, your neighbor was murdered...."

"Oh." Her lashes flutter. "Right." When she looks up at me, I can tell what I said has struck a nerve. With a quiver in her voice, she asks, "Should I be worried? Am I in danger?"

"My professional opinion is no, you're not in danger, but we don't know everything yet." Pointing at my card, I say, "If you're concerned about anything, call me."

"All right. I will."

"Good."

Grabbing the doorknob, I pull her door open and step into the hallway. Turning back, I watch her door shut and listen for her to lock it. When the familiar click sounds, I move back over to Kara's apartment. Police tape is crisscrossed over her doorway, and someone has placed a bouquet of flowers at the threshold. Bending at the waist, I look for a card or something indicating who set them here. When I don't spot anything, I turn back and look at Daisy's door.

Her muffled voice sounds from behind the thin wood. "No, I don't know who left the flowers."

I want to laugh at her response. She must have read the look on my face. "Thanks."

Once I'm outside of the complex, I pull my phone out of my pocket and press the button to stop the recording. Since she wouldn't let me take notes, I chose to record our conversation. Because I didn't notify her of that, it'd be inadmissible, but at least I'll be able to make my notes with more accuracy.

With that, I'm off to find something to eat. I'm starving. Then I need a good night's sleep.

CHAPTER FOUR

Gage

Sleep eludes me. Too many things are whirling around in my head, which sucks because that means I'll have gone a couple of day without decent sleep. It can't be helped. All I can think about is Kara Becker's murder. Looking at the clock on my nightstand, I see I've got time to get a workout in, shower, and get to the station before they take Tayler over to the courthouse for her arraignment. I'm not due to work until three o'clock this afternoon, but I feel the need to get there early. Perhaps Tayler will be able to answer a few questions that are nagging at me. I'll have to be careful about it, because I don't want to piss off Detective Trumbull, but I think Tayler will tell me things she wouldn't say to Dan. At least I hope so.

After a five-mile run, I shower, then grab a large coffee and breakfast sandwich from a drive-through. I'm good to go. The jog was good for a couple of reasons: it woke me up and also cleared my head some. The harder my feet beat down on the ground in a steady rhythm, the more I realized Quinn and the other Beedle women were right—Tayler isn't capable of killing someone. Threatening Kara? Yes, definitely. Now the question is how do I prove it? One way would be finding out what they discovered yesterday during the search of Tayler and Quinn's place yesterday. Dan had a search warrant executed. If Tayler swung that club, there would be, at the very least, blood traces on clothing and shoes. Some of the results from that search should be available today. If they took any of Tayler's property to forensics, I'll be able to find that out as well.

Which leaves me with Tayler. I need to get to her before the arraignment. I press on the gas to get to the station quicker.

~

"THANKS FOR AGREEING TO TALK TO ME, TAYLER."

The captain saw me the minute I stepped into the station and did the unexpected—he asked me to see if Tayler would talk to me since she and I knew each other. Now we're in one of the interrogation rooms, like the ones you see on television with the two-way glass. Captain Billings and Dan Trumbull are on the other side, watching from what we call "the booth."

"I need to get out of here, Gage." Tayler looks tired, pale, and honestly, shaken. I don't blame her.

I decide to just go for broke. "An eyewitness places you at Kara Becker's door just after ten the night of the murder."

Tayler sits back in the hard chair, places her hands in her lap, and slumps her shoulders. "I went there to tell her to stay away from Quinn."

"Tell me what happened. Start at the beginning."

She leans forward slightly. "Robbi sent me a text telling me she'd spotted Kara at Cy's."

I nod, already knowing about that.

"I knew Quinn was coming back soon, so I wanted to be sure Kara knew to stay away from her." She sighs. "So I found her address online and decided to pay her a visit."

"Was the night of the murder the first time you'd been to her apartment?"

"No." She shakes her head. "I'd tried two other times, but she was never there."

"Until *that* night?"

"Yeah. That night, I knocked, and she opened the door right away."

Tayler stops speaking, so I urge her on. "What happened next?"

"She said, 'Hey, Tayler.'" She blinks. "Which was weird and sort of overly familiar because she doesn't, or, I mean, she didn't really know me."

There's a long pause. I attempt to stay quiet, but she's taking too long between thoughts. "What did you say to that?"

"I said "hey" back." Tayler chuckles softly.

The room is silent again. Before I can nudge her to continue, Tayler does it on her own. "Then she shocked the crap out of me by inviting me into her place."

That is surprising.

"What did you do?"

Shrugging, she says, "I went in, and she shut the door."

Now, I need to know where she went in the apartment. If she touched anything. "Did you go into the living area? The kitchen? Her bedroom?" Hopefully fingerprints will come back later today, and we can either verify her claim or not.

"No." She shakes her head. "I didn't go any farther than her little hallway, right by the kitchen." I nod. Now Tayler's got her elbows on the table, and she's leaning closer. "She was cooking something."

The pasta that was burned dry in the pan. "Okay. What happened next?"

"I told her I'd heard she was back in town." Tayler leans back again. "And that she needed to go back home and leave Quinn alone."

"How did she respond to that?"

"Like a bitch." Tayler shakes her head. "I shouldn't say that. The poor girl is dead."

Once again, I keep my mouth shut. She's talking, and the more she does, the more we learn.

Tayler's eyes are glassy, like tears are close to the edge. When she looks up at me and blinks, one lone droplet hits her cheek. "She wasn't a nice person. I didn't like her, but I didn't *kill* her. She was very much alive when I left."

"You didn't tell me what she said to you after you asked her to leave Ames."

Wiping her cheek, she sighs. "She told me to worry about my own fucking problems, that it was none of my business and that Quinn was fat and pathetic."

I wince at the last quote. "Did she say anything else?"

"Sh-She said I was lucky someone like Luke Green would give me the time of day because she'd heard I was, erm, a cold fish."

A cold fish? I've heard the expression before, but it's strange hearing it from a twenty-one-year-old. "So she knew about your relationship with Luke?"

"I guess." She shrugs.

That's interesting. Kara had been gone for a while. "How do you think she found out about the two of you?"

"She may have seen us together. I don't know."

"What do you think she meant by 'cold fish'?"

"I took it to mean in, um, bed."

"Sexually?" I ask without thinking. "Why would she say something like that?"

"I have *no* idea." Tayler's head moves from side to side. "Seriously. No idea."

"What else was said? By either of you?"

"Not much. It was awkward. I could tell she wanted me to leave. She just stood there glaring at me with her hands on her hips, so I just shrugged, opened the door, and left."

"What time did you leave the victim's apartment?"

"I don't know, but I couldn't have been there more than ten minutes or so. I mean, it was pointless. I knew the girl wasn't going to listen to me."

Then why go there? "Where did you go next?"

"Home. I got into my pajamas and did some homework."

"What time was that?"

"I think I opened my books at around ten thirty or eleven. I sent Luke a text at about the same time, so I can check that and let you know."

I'm sure we've already requested her text messages and phone records. That's one of the first things they would have done yesterday along with the warrant to search her apartment.

"Okay, well, thanks, Tayler. You were really helpful."

"Can I go now?" Her voice breaks a little at the question.

"You'll need to wait until the arraignment to see what the judge says."

"Oh shit." The tears start to fall in rapid succession. I reach behind me and pick up a box of tissues we've got in the room for just this type of thing.

"It's gonna be okay, Tayler."

"H-How do you kn-know?"

"If you're innocent, our investigation will find the real killer." At least I hope so. I believe her, which means someone else bludgeoned Kara Becker, and it's our job to find them.

I watch as Tayler's escorted from the interrogation room back to the holding cell. Once she's out, Dan and the captain step in.

"Her story checks out," Dan mumbles. "We were able to track her phone movements through pings, and her timetable was right."

"That's good." I probably shouldn't be expressing any feelings about this one way or another, but the captain is well aware of my friendship with Tayler.

"That doesn't mean she didn't whack her with a golf club,"

Dan retorts. "Her little visit coincides with the time of death the coroner gave us."

I sigh. "Well, *I* believe her."

CHAPTER FIVE

Gage

Some nights last forever. Like tonight. I'm dog tired, and there's nothing going on in the city of Ames, Iowa. Hell, no one is even speeding. I guess that's due to the fact that it's the middle of the week and it's after three in the morning. No matter, it's my job to patrol whatever part of town they assign me.

Deciding to pull into a convenience store to grab another cup of coffee, I park the car near the front entrance, unbuckle my belt, and am about to step out of my cruiser when my personal cell phone rings. Reaching over, I pick it up from the passenger seat. I don't recognize the caller. Hitting the green dot, I say, "Golden."

"Um," a soft voice says, "Officer Golden?" I can barely hear her, she's whispering so softly.

"Yes. This is Officer Golden."

"Um... it's Daisy. Daisy Buchanan from—"

"What is it, Daisy? Are you okay?"

"S-Someone's inside Kara's apartment."

I buckle my belt and start my cruiser. "They're trying to break into her place?"

"Yeah. Well, I think so."

"Okay. Make sure your door's locked. I'm three minutes away."

"Thank you."

I hang up and call it in. "10-66. 1320 Coconino Road, number 2-1-3. Backup needed."

I wait for a response from dispatch. "10-4. 10-66. 1320 Coconino Road, number 2-1-3. Officer requests backup."

I listen for a beat more until she says, "ETA five minutes."

I flip on my cherries but leave the sirens off. I'd prefer whoever's trying to break into Kara Becker's place to not hear me coming. As soon as I get within sight of the complex, I turn off the flashing lights before I pull in.

I know I should wait for backup, but if I don't get up there, the suspect could be gone. I jump out of my car and head toward the entrance. Pulling my weapon from my holster, I open the door and press my back to the wall next to it. Peeking inside, I see no one. I do the same both entering and exiting the stairwell. As quietly as possible, I make my way down the hallway toward number 213. When I get close enough, I notice the police tape has been pulled down and her door is ajar. "Gotcha," I mutter to myself.

At Kara's door, I lean back against the wall and listen. I hear someone inside. How could I miss it? They're so loud with what sounds like doors opening and closing and drawers slamming shut. Whoever's inside isn't worried about getting caught.

Just then, I catch movement to my left. Glancing that way, I see my backup has arrived. Officer Finch is back—*hurray*—and he's not alone. He's with his training partner, Sergeant Jane Montgomery. At least one of them knows what they're doing.

With a wave, they both turn and place their backs against the wall. Using my fingers, I count to three. On three, I move quickly, kicking the door open and entering Kara's apartment with my gun drawn. When I see our perp, I recognize him immediately. Dylan Forrester.

"Stop. Police," I shout. When he turns, I yell, "Put your hands above your head."

But the idiot just stands there like a deer in headlights.

"Now," I say in my most commanding voice. When the guy finally does it, I sigh in relief but only for myself. "Don't move. Keep your hands above your head."

That's when the rookie swoops in, grabs one of Forrester's hands, and brings it behind his back to cuff him.

"Are you aware that this is a crime scene?" I ask with gritted teeth.

He nods. "I n-needed something."

"What? What did you need?" This kind of shit makes me crazy. Respect the police tape, asshole.

He shakes his head. "Nothin'."

I'm not going to bother asking him anything else right now, so I read him his Miranda rights and watch as Finch and Montgomery take him to the stairs to their car. Then they'll take the guy down to the station for questioning. I'll need to follow them down there soon so I can ask him some questions of my own. Namely what was Tayler Sorenson's ex-boyfriend doing in Kara Becker's apartment?

Before I head out, though, I need to check on Daisy. She sounded terrified on the phone. I raise my hand to knock on her door, but before I can make contact, it's pulled open and a very disheveled Daisy Buchanan stands before me.

"Did you get him?" she asks timidly.

Why do I think she already knows the answer to that question? She seems to be aware of everything that's going on at Kara's place.

"He's in custody."

She sighs with relief. "Okay. Good."

I'm not sure why, but I ask, "Mind if I ask you a few questions?"

"No." She opens the door the rest of the way. "Come on in."

Stepping into Daisy's apartment, I notice something has changed. "You got rid of the boxes?" The ones that were blocking the sliding glass doors that lead to the deck are gone.

"Oh, yeah. I finally went through it all."

I can't help my next question. "How long had they been there?"

"A while." She shrugs. "I've just been, erm, busy."

Which reminds me. "What do you do, Daisy?"

She blinks at me, and I realize it's the first time I've seen her without her giant glasses. Her eyes are large, yes, but the big eyewear must magnify them some. But now I can see her eye color. I was right to say gray, but in her incandescent lights, I'd say her eyes were more steel gray. No matter, she looks... pretty. *Very* pretty.

She blinks several times before she speaks. "For a job, you mean?"

"Yes. What do you do for a job?"

"Oh, um, I work from home."

"You do? What do you do?"

"Research."

Wow, getting information from this girl is like pulling teeth.

"What kind of research?"

"You aren't going to let this go, are you?" Daisy's got her hands on her hips and a scowl on his face.

I chuckle. "I guess not." I mean, what's the big deal?

"Fine." She scoffs. "I work for my dad."

"Your dad?" I thought she didn't like her father. At least that's the impression I got the last time we spoke.

"He writes articles and papers. You know, 'publish or perish,' as they say in academia."

I've never heard that expression before. I may have to do a little search later. "So, you research for your father."

She shrugs. "Yeah."

I want to ask her if that's a full-time gig, because if not, I'm curious how she affords this place. It isn't cheap.

Deciding to return to the topic at hand, I say, "So, the guy who just broke into Kara's place. You see him before?"

Daisy gives me one nod. "He's been here a few times that I've seen, so probably more."

"Was he living here?" She probably won't be able to answer that question, but Dylan can.

She shrugs, and that's all I get from her.

It doesn't matter if he lived with her. He's suspect number two, which will help Tayler out immensely. Now we just need to find out what Dylan was up to.

Another good question: How long has he known Kara Becker, and *if* he killed her, what would be his motive?

CHAPTER SIX

Daisy

The second I saw that guy going into Kara's apartment, I knew it was my chance to see Officer Golden again. The thought of it made me both nervous and excited. And scared. I mean, not a soul has stepped foot in my place for almost two years.

Except my dad.

But he doesn't count.

For anything.

Since he's paying my rent, he thinks he can dictate who I can have in my apartment, which is nobody, because he wants to keep what I'm doing here a dirty little secret. He's also got a key to the place, so I can't very well say *he* can't stop by—especially when he's here to pick up his "research." And by research, I mean his articles, books, and anything else he's published in the last six years. Yes, I've been doing all of his writing since I graduated high school.

It all started rather harmlessly. One night, back when I had a relationship with him, Dad and I were eating dinner, and we began talking about Ernest Hemingway. Since he's one of my favorite authors, I'd done quite a bit of reading on him. More than my dad had, apparently, because we spent the entire meal arguing the secret meaning behind *The Old Man and the Sea*, my favorite story of Hemingway's. My dad got angry with me and told me to "prove it." So I did. I wrote a paper on Hemingway's story along with my theories on the symbolism he used throughout and backed it up with thorough research.

After I handed him the paper, he read it and smiled. "Send me your file, would you?" By that, he meant he wanted my digital document file. I didn't think anything of it. I assumed he was going to edit what I wrote. Little did I know he changed my name at the top of the paper to his and submitted it to a prestigious journal on American literature. He won an award for that article. Not only that, it helped him finally get tenure, something he'd been working toward for years. Now he's seen as a "leading authority on Hemingway". I want to scream whenever I see that printed because Dad *hates* Hemingway. F. Scott Fitzgerald is his favorite. My name, the one he insisted upon, should have been your first clue. And it makes my skin crawl because Daisy Buchanan, from *The Great Gatsby*, was a bitch.

So that's how it started. In exchange for my apartment and a little spending money, I write for him. Even while I was getting my own degree, I kept writing for him. My most recent project, the one I'm currently writing, is an entire book about Hemingway. It's also my chance to get away from here, from my dad. This will be my last project for Dr. Dorian Buchanan. After this, he's on his own, and I'll be set free. Because I've got plans of my own, and they don't include my father.

You see, I've got a few secrets of my own.

AFTER OFFICER GOLDEN—*GAGE*—LEAVES MY APARTMENT, I contemplate going to bed, but since I'm not tired, I opt to start going through the containers that hold all of the newspapers and magazines that have been stacked around my place ever since my mom left. They really are hers; she asked me to keep them for her until she got back from her "little trip." She's been gone five years, ever since the day she found out dad was using my writing for his own advancement. I guess that was the last straw for her. I'm not surprised. They hadn't been getting along—not for a while.

I don't blame her, really. Dad's career always came before anything else. I suspect she was tired of being second or even third fiddle. We used to be a family. Before my dad became obsessed with his career, the three of us used to do things together. We used to laugh. But something happened to Dad along the way that changed him. Maybe it was his own need to outdo his father, the late great Dr. Rochester Buchanan. Who knows?

Interestingly enough, they aren't actually divorced. Dad's tried to get her to sign papers, but she's never in a place long enough to have anything delivered.

Long story short, that's why I have her stuff. She asked me to hold on to all of it for her, and that's what I've done for years, but I'm tired of it. Of *all* of it. I'm tired of being a tool they both use. For Dad, I do his work, and for Mom, I keep her crap.

Well, no more.

I look over at the tall stack of magazines I've pulled from two plastic bins. I step closer, trying to decide where to start. I know some of these are worth money. Take the very first *Vogue* magazine published in 1892. It's one of my mom's most prized possessions. I won't toss that, but most of the other stuff, yes, definitely.

I sigh looking at the stacks. I wish she were here to do this. Not only that, more than anything, I miss her. I want her back, and I guess I thought holding on to all her things would help draw her back. But living like a hoarder isn't good for anyone. God, how many times has my dad threatened to come in here while I was gone to toss her stuff away? Maybe I should have let him do it. At least she'd be angry with *him* instead of me. It'd put the onus of guilt on the man who caused this mess in the first place. That is *if* she ever comes back. I thought it was my duty—no, my *responsibility* to hold on to her things. If she didn't want to see *me*, she'd at least want her precious *Vogue* magazine. But, like the clothing hanging on the rack next to my kitchen and the crates with her miscellaneous housewares, it's all got to go.

I've lived like a hermit long enough. While I leave my apartment to get groceries and things of that nature, I mostly stick around home to make sure... well, I never know when my dad's going to let himself into my place, so I like to be here, just in case.

Now I've got something else to keep me tethered to my apartment. I mean, what if something happens at Kara's place? If I'm away, who'll call Gage?

A small smile crawls across my face because Gage Golden is... well, I think he may be perfect.

CHAPTER SEVEN

Gage

I make my way back to the station after talking with Daisy. I want to observe Dylan Forrester's questioning.

The first person I see upon entering is my captain. "Good job tonight. You caught the kid trying to break into Kara's place. Name's Dylan—"

"Forrester. I know him."

The captain chuckles. "I'm not surprised."

I don't know what he means by that. Probably because I know the other players in this drama too. "He's Tayler Sorenson's ex-boyfriend. The one who was stalking her."

Captain Billings scratches his chin. "So the two of them are working together."

"The two? Which two?"

"Sorenson and Forrester."

What the hell is he talking about? "Doubtful since Sorenson pressed charges against him *and* has a no-contact order on the guy." Choosing to move on, I ask, "Who's questioning him?"

"You."

I shake my head. "Not a good idea. I brought him in for the stalking. He's not gonna talk to me. Where's Trumbull?"

"He's not coming in today."

He's off? In the middle of a murder investigation.

"Which means it's either you or Finch."

"Captain—"

"I'll be in the booth if you run into trouble."

Great.

"They're bringing him down now, so get your ducks in a row, Golden."

Fuck the ducks. He's not giving me any time to prep for this. It's not going to go well.

"By the way, I want Finch in there with ya. He needs to learn how to talk to suspects."

Awesome.

"WHAT WERE YOU DOING IN KARA'S APARTMENT, DYLAN?" I may as well start right off with that question because we need to know why he was there in the first place.

"I already told you. I went to get my stuff."

"What stuff?"

"*My* stuff, man. I was crashing at her place."

"Crashing?"

"Jesus, dude. She let me stay there."

"I didn't realize you knew Kara Becker. How long have you been staying with her?"

He shrugs. "A couple of weeks."

"You had a key?" I assume because he didn't break into the apartment. There was no damage to the door.

"Yeah, man. She gave me a key because I. Was. Staying. There."

Wow, this kid is beyond belligerent. "Watch yourself," I growl. I hate punks like this. "Were you seeing her... romantically?"

Dylan laughs. "You mean, was I fucking her?"

"If that's how you'd prefer the question. Were you?"

He chuckles again. "You can't say 'fuck' or something, dude?"

"Answer the question."

Dylan makes a scoffing sound, and I roll my hand into a fist. Damn, I'd love to punch him. "Sure, we fucked a time or two, but we weren't *together*, if you know what I mean."

"Why not?"

"What the hell, man? What's your obsession with my sex life?"

Now I laugh right along with Finch. But why is *he* laughing? "Asking you about your relationship with the deceased isn't about your sex life, Mr. Forrester. It's about who murdered her."

"Fuck. It wasn't me, man. I was partying that night. *All* night," Dylan adds with a smirk.

"I see you've provided us with some names of people who can corroborate your whereabouts the night of the murder."

He nods, then smiles.

"We'll get them in here so they can answer some questions as well."

His smile drops.

"So, back to my earlier question. Why weren't you and Kara in a relationship?"

"She had too many irons in the fire, if you know what I mean."

Irons? Interesting turn of a phrase, considering.

He continues, "No time for anything more than just a fuck or two. Same with me. I'm still in lo—I still have feelings for someone else."

Tayler.

I nod. "Sure. I get it. Did you know they arrested Tayler Sorenson for Kara's murder?"

"I'd heard something like that." He shrugs.

"Do you think she did it?"

"Nah. She's too...."

I wait for more, but he's just sitting there, so I ask, "What? She's too what?"

"Prissy. She'd never do something like that. It'd be too messy."

Of all the reasons to think someone wouldn't kill another person, that's a first. "Too messy?"

"Yeah, you know, blood. Tayler wouldn't be able to handle the mess."

Funny thing about a crime of passion, people don't think about the mess. Not until it's too late. "What *irons* did Kara Becker have in the fire?"

From the expression on his face, I'd say he knows things that he's not sure he should tell me.

"She's gone, Dylan. This information could help us find her killer." *Assuming you're not it, dickface.*

"She... she needed money."

I arch my brow. "Wasn't her father helping her anymore?"

He shrugs. "She needed *more* money."

"Why?"

"She wanted to get out of here. You know, head to California or some shit."

And what was the source of this additional money?"

"I... I think she was using information she had on people to—"

"Blackmail?"

"No." He shakes his head. "Not really. She just knew stuff. People would pay her for the info."

That's blackmail, idiot. This makes no sense. "Give me an example."

"I don't have one."

"Come on, Dylan. You know something." I know he does.

"The only thing I remember was about some dude having an affair. She was going to tell if he didn't pay." Adding a little snort, he says, "And the dude had *bank*."

Jesus. So the guy was loaded. "That's called blackmail, Dylan." And it breaks this case wide open. "Do you have a name?"

He shakes his head. "No. I had nothing to do with that shit."

Deciding to change directions, I ask him, "When did you meet Kara?" He just stares at me quietly. Still thinking about the blackmail, perhaps. "Dylan?"

"I don't remember."

That's not going to fly. "Was it last semester? Last year?"

Still nothing.

"Let's try this. *Where* did you meet her?"

"Cy's." He pauses. "I think."

Cy's is Cy's Roost, a popular college bar and hangout right next to the Iowa State University campus. The same place Robbi spotted Kara. It's also owned by Tayler Sorenson's boyfriend, Luke Green. "You met at Luke's bar?"

He growls at my question, so I rephrase it. "Was this *before* Tayler began seeing Luke Green?"

"Yes. No." Dylan shakes his head and replies angrily, "I don't fucking remember."

"Would you say you've known the victim for a year?" I wait for a reaction from him but get nothing. "Six months?"

"Jesus." He starts fidgeting in his seat, clearly agitated. "Something like that. Yeah, about six or seven months."

"So, around the time you were stalking Tayler, you met Kara?"

"I wasn't fucking stalking her," he growls, angrily.

Ignoring his false claim, I rephrase. "You met at Cy's Roost around the time you were trying to get back together with Tayler?"

He leans forward in his chair, runs a hand into his hair, and pulls at it. Hard. "What the hell... fuck, man. Yes. What's the big deal?"

He's getting more and more twitchy. Interesting. "Just want to be sure I've got all the information I need."

"For what?" Dylan's out of his seat and pounding on the table now.

Finch races to the other side of the table and places a hand on Dylan's shoulder and neck, shouting, "Sit the fuck down."

Dylan flops back into his chair and does that thing with his hair again. "Man, I don't get it. What'd I do wrong?"

"You entered an apartment that's considered a crime scene."

"I told you. Jesus. I needed my shit."

"Uh-huh." I look down at the inventory sheet from Kara Becker's apartment. "What were you looking for exactly?"

"My shit."

"So you've said." I push the sheet in front of him. "Which of these items were you looking for?"

I bet Finch a hundred bucks I knew what he was after. I'm just waiting for him to tell me he needed his bag of weed and pot paraphernalia that was sitting on Kara's coffee table. While it's legal in some states, Iowa isn't one of them. Not yet, anyway.

He leans over and reads through the list. When he gets to the alphabetized M section, he looks up at me. "It's for medicinal purposes."

"Iowa doesn't have medical marijuana." We've got cannabidiol, but it's only for specific diagnoses.

"Shit." Dylan drags his hand through his hair again. Then, like a lightbulb just flashed in his head, he looks up at me and smiles. Pointing at the page, he says, "The weed wasn't mine. It was Kara's."

Wow, that's a shitty thing to do. Blame the victim. "Well, if that wasn't it, then what 'shit' were you looking for?"

He glances down at the list of items from Kara Becker's apartment. "My toiletries."

"Uh-huh." I push my chair back and stand. Looking at the rookie, I say, "Finch, take him back to the holding cell."

"What!" Dylan screeches. "Why can't I leave? I was just getting my shit."

Ignoring him, I step out of the room and spot the captain drinking a cup of coffee and staring at the two-way glass. Once the door shuts, he smiles. "Nice job, Golden."

I'm not sure what was so 'nice' about that. "I didn't get much."

"We now know he and Becker were friends for longer than a couple of weeks."

Which is odd. How and why did the two of them decide to be friends? One hated Quinn, the other was obsessed with Tayler.

The captain makes a humming noise before he asks, "What would Becker get out of befriending someone like that dipshit Forrester?"

That's an interesting question. "She hated Quinn. Quinn and Tayler are best friends. My guess? She had more plans to make Quinn's life uncomfortable."

"You should have asked him about that." The captain is right.

I turn and peer through the glass, watching as Finch escorts Dylan from the room. Before I have the chance to think it through, I open the door back up. "Dylan?"

He stops and turns, anger written all over his face. "What?"

"Did Kara approach you first, or was it the other way around?"

He blinks at me.

"When you met at Cy's for the first time. Did she approach you?"

"Yeah." He nods. "Yeah, she did."

"I need you to think about this. Did she know who you were?" He's staring at me. "Do you remember what she said to you?"

Dylan raises his head and lowers it slowly. "She asked me...." He swallows visibly. "She asked me if I wanted to get Tayler back."

Okay. This is getting weird. "What did she mean?"

Turning toward me, Dylan steps back into the room. "She said she'd help me get Tayler back."

"Why?"

He shrugs. "I don't know."

"And did she? Help you?"

The look on Dylan's face reminds me of the times my little brother was caught doing something he shouldn't have been. "She did surveillance."

"Surveillance?"

"On Tayler. She took the photos. Most of 'em."

"She was in Ames? Helping you?" Her dad promised he'd do his best to keep Kara out of Ames after the incidents with Quinn Maxwell. It was either that or Quinn was going to press charges. "Was she staying in her apartment at that time?"

"Off and on. Her dad made her come home sometimes."

So Dad knew. Interesting.

If his daughter weren't dead, I'd have him in here to answer a few questions. But now's not the time for that.

"Thanks, Dylan." I turn to head back into the booth.

"Can I leave now?" His voice is calmer than before.

"That's up to the captain. I'll see what I can do."

"All right."

When I hear the door click closed, I move into the booth with the captain as he mutters, "That little girl was up to no good."

I know he's referring to Kara, and I think he's right. "Did you hear Dylan say she had 'a bunch of irons in the fire'?" I shake my head. "Blackmail."

The captain nods and chews on what looks to be a cookie. Where'd he get a cookie? "You'll need to go through her place with a fine-tooth comb. See if she's got anything there that can help us figure out who she was extracting money from."

"Me? What about Trumbull?"

"He's got some personal, er, stuff going on."

I arch my brow and wait for more.

He sighs. "His wife's fucking around on him. His head isn't in the game."

"And?" What does this all mean to me?

"And congratulations," he deadpans. "You're now the detective in charge of this case."

"But—"

"Now get to work." And with that, he's up and out of the booth before I can say another word.

I sure as hell hope I get a raise for this.

CHAPTER EIGHT

Gage

Fortunately—or unfortunately, depending on how you look at it—Finch gets assigned to help me with the case since Detective Trumbull is AWOL. The captain decided to release Dylan, warning him to stay away from Kara Becker's apartment. Hopefully he passed along the same advice as it relates to Tayler. She's out on bail thanks to Luke, so Dylan needs to stay far away from her as well. And with the new information from Forrester, Tayler has a good shot at fighting the charges. Hopefully her lawyer's good enough to see the evidence against Tayler is circumstantial at best. With Dylan's knowledge about Kara attempting to blackmail at least one person, her chances are even better.

That's where Finch and I start off our day—trying to figure out who Kara was extorting by searching her apartment again. The initial search was more superficial. The team gathered fibers, got fingerprints from every surface, took a multitude of photographs, etc. Now Finch and I are going through her place with a fine-tooth comb, and while we're here, Detective Dan has decided to put in a day's work as well. He's going through all of Becker's social media accounts, phone records including text messages, and the stuff we got from her car, including a journal she had in her glove box.

"Sir," Finch says from her bedroom. I gave him the task of going through that room, making sure not to leave any stone unturned because you'd be surprised where people hide stuff. Example: The freezer is a common hiding place, as are the backs and bottoms of drawers.

"Yeah?" I say from the kitchen.

"Found something."

Stepping into the bedroom, my feet sound like I'm walking on dry leaves thanks to the shoe covers I've got on. Rubber gloves and a hair covering help round out the outfit. "Whatcha got?"

Finch has the mattress pushed off the bed. It's now leaning against the wall. He points to the platform bed, where a manila envelope, one about nine by eleven inches, has been hidden between two boards. He's right. He found something.

"Let's take photos before you extract it." Pulling my phone from my back pocket, I take pics of the slats on the platform then back up and take more shots from different angles. "Okay." I nod.

I watch as Finch carefully tugs at the corner until it slides free. Bending the metal closure, he opens the top and peers inside. "Photos." He turns the envelope over, the contents landing on the bed frame. As he leans in, I step closer. Using his gloved hand, Finch spreads them out farther so we can see each one.

Finch speaks first. "Weird that these are printed out." On photo paper, no less. "These days, it's all digital files."

"Hmm. True. For effect, maybe."

"Huh?"

I stare down at six eight-by ten-inch photos. Three include images of a man and a woman. You can't see the woman, only her arms and legs, but it's obvious what they're doing. "You know, I bet she printed them off so she could mail them or show them without having her camera or phone grabbed. Plus, a hard copy is going to have more impact. For effect," I repeat so he understands what I mean.

"So, who are they?"

"No idea." I lean closer to the images. "The guy's older." I point to the hair.

"They're in some kind of office." Finch looks up at me, then back down. "There's a desk and some bookshelves."

"Yep." And it's obvious what they're doing since the man's pants are down around his ankles.

Finch pushes the top three photos aside to reveal two images of Tayler with Luke. They're kissing in one and holding hands in another. I bet those pissed off Dylan. The last image has the same effect on me because this one is of Quinn Maxwell. She's sitting alone in what looks like the HUB on the Iowa State's central campus. She's looking at a book as she bites into something, a pastry of some kind. Standing up to my full height, I tell Finch to "Bag and tag everything including the envelope" before adding, "We'll need fingerprints done on that." I turn to head back into the kitchen but stop. "Good job, Finch. Let's keep going."

"Right, sir."

Sir? That's the second time he's called me that. Maybe I was wrong about Finch.

As I'm about to return to my kitchen search, a knock sounds on the door. Without thinking, I step up and open it. "Daisy?"

"Oh, um...," she starts nervously. "I, uh, saw you go into her apartment. I thought I'd see if you needed anything."

I blink a few times, wondering if that's all this woman does—watches out her door. "No. I think we're good."

"Oh. Right." She titters nervously. "It's just... I made some cookies."

"Cookies?" says the guy I thought "wasn't so bad" a minute ago. Poking his head out from the bedroom, Finch sees Daisy and smiles, and it pisses me off. "Did you say cookies?"

"I did." *Why is she smiling at Finch?* "When you take a break, just knock on my door and I'll have some ready for you."

"Awesome." Finch's huge smile is ridiculous.

Shutting the door, I glare at him. "You act like you've never had food before." The jackass.

"Homemade cookies?" He smiles again. "I haven't had home-made cookies in months."

Come to think of it, neither have I.

"Just keep working," I grunt.

"Then we get cookies, yeah?"

"Yeah," I mumble. "Then we get cookies."

CHAPTER NINE

Daisy

I can't believe I just said that. "I made cookies," I say in a squeaky voice, making fun of myself. Ugh. I'm such an idiot. I could tell by Gage's face that he wasn't happy for the interruption. Hell, he looked downright angry about it.

"Stupid, stupid Daisy."

Well, damn it, it couldn't be helped. I heard voices in the hallway. Male voices. And I had to check it out—like I always do. When I saw him, I knew I had to do *something*. Not to mention I'd been meaning to make cookies. I've had all the ingredients for days, after all.

No. I'm not going to beat myself up about it. Mom always said, "A way to a man's heart is through his stomach." For a long time, I didn't understand what she meant. I thought it meant if a man needed heart surgery, the doctor had to cut through the stomach first, but as I got older and read more, I realized it was merely a figure of speech. She didn't mean it literally.

So that's what I did, or at least what I'm trying to do. Or at least I *tried* to get to his heart with food. But, the two words I'd use to describe how that worked out?

Epic. Fail.

With a self-pitying sigh, I place the finished cookies in a plastic container and clean up my mess. I should have known he wasn't interested in me *that* way. He's just doing his job, and I happen to be a person who pays attention to what goes on around here. No doubt Officer Golden probably has a slew of women making him cookies.

"Ugh. So embarrassing."

Why do I do things like that to myself?

My last crush was.... I have to stop to think. My last crush was in high school. Chad Esther. He was in my precalculus class and was a wiz at math. Me, not so much. I passed it by the skin of my teeth. I really wanted to ask him to tutor me. I knew he struggled in English composition a little, so we could have helped each other out, but I chickened out. No matter. I heard he was married now, to a man. So there's that. I hope he's happy. I really do. He was nice.

Now there's Gage. I can't very well ask him to tutor me. I snort aloud at my thought. "I made cookies," I say again as I roll my eyes. "You are such a dork, Daisy."

WITH MY KITCHEN TIDIED UP, I DECIDE TO WORK ON DAD'S book for a while. I'm nearly finished, thank goodness. Once it's completed and edited, I need to figure out a way to break the news to my father that I'm done. I won't be writing any more papers or books for him. Instead, I'll be focusing on *my* plan—*my* goals. He's not going to like it, but too bad.

I'm able to concentrate on the writing for about an hour before turning back to Mom's crap I was working on before making the cookies. I pull up my tall stool to continue. I've found the original *Vogue* magazine and several others published around the same time. Those I placed into a plastic container for safe-keeping. The other, less important items, I've tossed into large black garbage bags. I've filled one and nearly have a second one ready to throw out when there's a knock on my door.

I'm immediately excited because it has to be Gage. Hopping off my stool, I make my way to the door. "Just a second," I say in a singsong kind of voice. But when I pull the door open, my smile disappears.

"Dad? What are you doing here?"

I don't wait for an answer, just turn on my heel and make my way into the apartment, leaving the door open for him.

He shuts it on his way inside. "Wow, nice greeting, Daisy Fay."

I hate when he uses my first *and* middle name.

"What're you up to? Been writing?" His voice is all cheery and fake because he's hoping I've been working on his book.

"Some."

I sit on the tall stool and continue looking at each item in the stack to decide if it's a keeper or not.

I feel him next to me, watching me as I lean over and throw something away. "You finally getting rid of your mother's shit?"

Ignoring him would be ideal, but that's impossible with Dorian Buchanan. "Going through it all."

"You've gotten rid of the boxes. Good." From the corner of my eye, I see him nod. "Having all of that crap in here makes you look like a crazy person."

Ignore him, Daisy. "Uh-huh" is all I say.

He moves to my desk and sits in my office chair, then wiggles the mouse to wake up my computer. It's password protected, so he can't see what I've got on my computer. "You gonna show me what you've written in the last week?"

No. That's what I'd like to say, but it won't fly. Besides, the sooner I show him what I've got, the faster he'll leave. Tossing another magazine into the trash bag, I stand and make my way to the desk. I pause in front of him, waiting for him to give me my chair. He rises but doesn't go far, which makes me tense.

Typing in my password, I make a mental note to change it

again as soon as he leaves. Fortunately, the file is already open. Standing, I let him take the seat again so he can read what I've got. I know what'll happen next. He'll begin questioning some of my findings. He always does. *Always.* And 99 percent of the time, he's wrong. Every once in a while, he'll catch something I missed, but not very often.

"I'm not sure about this paragraph."

See?

"Which paragraph?" I ask as I reach for the folder that holds my research.

"This one, about Hemingway's sister, Ursula."

"What about her?" I already know what he's going to say.

"She didn't kill herself. She died of cancer."

Yes, she did kill herself, but arguing with my father does no good. Instead, I open my research folder and pull out the information on Ursula. "Here." I hand it to him. As he reads, I return to my stack.

"I'll be...," he mumbles to himself.

"Yep."

"What about—"

I don't know what he's going to question next because there's a knock on my door. I cringe.

No. Not now.

The last thing I want is my dad to see I've made cookies for someone. A man. But when the knock sounds again, I know I've got to get it before my father does.

Quickly, I make my way to the door. Peeking out the peephole, I don't see Gage. It's the other one. Sighing, I pull the door open and put a fake smile on my face. "Oh, hey." Like I'm surprised to see him.

"I can't stop thinking about the cookies," he says with a smile. It's a nice smile. Not as nice as Gage's but still....

"Sure."

I step into my kitchen to retrieve my plastic container when my dad hisses in my ear, "What the fuck is a cop doing here?"

First of all, even though my dad is a cheat and a liar, he rarely cusses.

"I made them cookies."

"Why is he *here*?"

"Oh." I can't believe my father doesn't know. "They're across the hall, investigating."

"Investigating what?" He's still whispering, sort of.

"My neighbor was murdered."

Dad's eyes grow round. "And you didn't bother to call me?"

I raise a brow. "Why would I?"

"Because, Daisy." He says my name with contempt. Like always. "You know why. You shouldn't be here."

"It's fine. Gage says—" Oops. I'm not going there.

"Gage? Who the hell is Gage?"

"I am."

We both turn to see the one and only Officer Gage Golden in all his police uniformed glory. Except he's not wearing the same uniform as he did the first night. No. Today he's in dress pants and shirt with a jacket. He looks nice.

"You just let yourself in?" my dad snaps.

"The door was open. Finch was inside." Gage shrugs. "Plus, Daisy sounded distressed."

I did?

"May I ask who you are, sir?" Gage asks.

"No," my dad says gruffly.

Not wanting this to get out of hand, I say quickly, "This is my father, Dr. Dorian Buchanan." He prefers I say the entire name. Hell, he prefers *everyone* say his entire name. The "doctor" part is very important to him.

"Right." Gage holds his hand out to my father, but Dad doesn't move. It's like he's refusing to shake it.

Doing my best to end this little standoff, I hand the entire container of cookies to Gage. "Here." It's sad, really. I love that container, but I can replace it. "Take these."

Gage reaches out and takes it. "You sure?"

"Positive."

"Thanks, Daisy."

From behind Gage, the other cop says, "Yeah. Thanks, Daisy."

"You're welcome."

I follow them both until they're out the door. Shutting it behind them, I close my eyes, waiting for what's to come. I don't have to wait too long.

"What the hell do you think you're doing, Daisy?"

"I don't know what you mean," I say as I turn to face him.

"Inviting strange men in here?" He points downward. "To *my* apartment?" The sneer on his face is ugly. Almost as ugly as he is in the inside. "I've warned you—"

"I know." I nod. "You'll stop paying for this place if I can't abide by your rules." Which is why I'm moving. As soon as this book is done, I'm out of here.

"That's right." He steps closer, lowering his voice as he goes. "I've warned you."

I nod. He has. Many times.

"And yet here you are inviting men into *my* home."

"I—" What? I'm not sure what to say in response. "I'm sorry." Don't judge. The only reason I said that was to hopefully end this conversation so he'll leave.

"You should be." Dad's voice softens. "You should have told me about your neighbor."

"It was on the news."

"You know I don't watch television."

No. My dad is one of those snobby people who thinks television is beneath him.

"I'm sure it was in the paper."

"Don't be impertinent, Daisy Fay."

"Sorry." *Not sorry. Please leave.*

"I need to go. I've got an interview."

Of course he does.

Moving toward the door, he reaches for the knob, then turns his head. "No more guests."

"Right." I nod. "I won't."

"Promise?" he asks, and it sounds nice, but it's actually loaded with something familiar.

"Promise." How will he know one way or the other? Hell, he didn't even know my neighbor was murdered. And trust me, *everyone* knew about the murder, because things like *that* don't happen in Ames, Iowa. Ever.

CHAPTER TEN

Gage

"What was with that guy?" Finch asks as he bites into another cookie.

"No idea." Well, I do. Daisy alluded to the fact that she and her dad weren't close. "There's something familiar about him."

Finch shrugs. "He looks like your average old white guy."

Old? I wouldn't call Dr. Buchanan old. Older, yes. From the little bit of gray in his hair and some wrinkles around his eyes, my guess is he's in his late forties or early fifties. But why argue with a kid who's twenty-three if he's a day? "Yeah." I reach for another cookie.

"These are damn good," Finch mumbles with his mouth full.

He's right. "They are." *Damn* good. It makes me wonder what else she's good at. You know, in the cooking arena.

"She's cute." Finch seems to think I appreciate his opinion or something.

"I hadn't noticed." Yes I had. Take today, for example. She had on another one of her giant sweatshirts, but this one sort of fell off one shoulder, revealing creamy skin and a black strap. It could have been a bra strap or one those tank tops women wear. Whatever it was, it was certainly distracting. Her shoulder looked narrow, and given the fact that she's rather short, I'm not surprised the rest of her is compact. Sometimes, when she moves, I've caught a glimpse of body beneath all that fabric and what I've seen makes me smile. Curves. At least my hope is she's got curves.

Hope? Why would I hope? I can't be thinking about Daisy Buchanan in any way other than as an eyewitness.

I make a scoffing sound, which makes the human garbage disposal stop chewing for the first time since I opened up the container and ask, "What?"

"Nothing." Replacing the lid, I point to the bedroom. "Let's keep going. I'd like to get home sometime tonight."

"Sure thing, boss."

WE DON'T FIND ANYTHING ELSE IN KARA BECKER'S apartment. That doesn't mean she didn't keep things elsewhere, of course. I'd love to go through her bedroom in her father's home, because we're missing a significant item: her computer. Everyone's got a computer. But I'll need to check with the captain about that. I'd hope Kara's father would give us access to her things at home, but who knows. He's been a constant figure at the station since Kara's death. He sits in the captain's office waiting for updates which is sad. I feel for him, I really do, but he needs to take a little responsibility for the way Kara was. His help is needed. I'd like to sit down with Mr. Becker to get his insight into Kara's activities the few months leading up to her death. There may be something he noticed that can help us understand her motives. I'd also like to know if he knew about her desire to move west.

Sitting on my couch, I'm about to eat the last of the cookies. I stare down at the empty plastic container and frown. I've eaten a dozen cookies since she handed them to me, and while I'm full as a tick, I could eat more.

"What did she put in these things?" I know they have chocolate chips and oatmeal. I also taste coconut along with some crunchy bits in them too. Nuts? Whatever it is, they taste like nothing I've ever eaten before. They're addictive.

Leaning my head back, I chew slowly so I can savor the last one. What Finch said was true for me too. It's been a long time since I've eaten anything homemade. Sure, I cook for myself, but it's nothing special and never anything sweet. I cook a protein and a vegetable almost every day. That's about it.

Sighing, I look at the empty container again. All that remains are crumbs. Maybe if I wash the container and give it back to her, she'll fill it up again.

What? It doesn't hurt to be optimistic.

CHAPTER ELEVEN

Daisy

"Hi?" I say it like it's a question because it is. Why is Gage Golden at my door at eight in the morning?

Not that I'm complaining.

"Hey." He smiles, and it lights up his whole face. He must be a morning person. Unlike me.

That's when I cringe remembering what I'm wearing. The world's oldest pajama pants and a tight tank top. No bra.

Sure, I should have thought through the opening of my door, but when I saw him through the peephole, I grabbed the doorknob and wrenched it open. No thinking done whatsoever.

Crossing my arms to hide my chest, I step behind the door a little bit. "Hi." This time it's not a question.

"I brought you back your container." Looking down, I see his outstretched hand. It's holding the now empty cookie container.

"Wow, you guys ate them all? Already?" Taking it from him, I hold it in front of my chest like a shield

With a sexy chuckle, Gage says, "I had to fight Finch for the last few."

I blush because, well, that was a cool thing for him to say. "You liked them?"

I'm holding my breath waiting to hear what he's about to say.

He leans in closer and lowers his voice like he's telling me a secret. "Those were the best damn cookies I've ever had, Daisy."

Holy shit-balls. Whenever he says my name, my nipples get hard. Sorry if that was a little too much info, but it's true. He says my name, and it's like I don't mind it. My name, that is. For years, ever since I read *The Great Gatsby*, I've hated my name. Like detested it. But that changed the day Gage Golden let it cross his lips—his sexy, sexy lips—so now I'd like to thank my father for the gift.

Wait... what?

No. I won't thank my father for any of that. I'll just be thankful he liked my cookies.

"Well, if you liked those, you should try my brownies."

What the hell am I thinking? I want to punch *myself* in the throat. *Pathetic much, Daisy?*

"Well, if you'd like anyone to taste test one of your recipes, I volunteer."

Wow. Wow-wow-wow. "How 'bout dinner?"

"Uh, what?" he stammers.

"I'll make you dinner."

"Oh." He moves back one giant step. The most giant step I've ever seen. "I don't think...."

"Right." I feel the heat on my cheeks. It's like fire. "Of course you wouldn't want that—"

"No." He shakes his head. "I would. It's just—" He looks to his left. Toward Kara's apartment.

"Oh. Okay. I see. The investigation."

Nodding, he says what I already know. "You're an eyewitness."

"Sure. Sure. I get it." Not really. I mean, I'm not a suspect. Right?

"But after?" Why does he suddenly sound so unsure? Is he just trying to make me feel better?

"No. You don't need to do that."

"I want to." A small smile crosses his lips. "I bet you're a great cook."

And there you have it. He's just hungry.

That fact sucks donkey balls.

"I'm an okay cook." I'm being modest. The fact is I'm a *great* cook. My mom taught me. But now's not the time to brag, especially when I'm lining up a pity date. *Yay, me.*

"So your dad didn't like me."

I'm caught off guard by his comment. "My dad doesn't like anyone in my apartment." *His* apartment.

"I suppose that's normal. But you're an adult."

"That's what my birth certificate says." I snort and regret it the minute it happens.

Gage steps closer to me, reversing the mammoth step he just took away from me. "Look, Daisy." His voice is tentative. I'm not sure I want to hear this. "I'd love to have dinner with you—after this case is solved."

The blush is back, but this time it's not because I'm embarrassed. No, this time the heat rising up from my center is for all the right reasons. "Okay." I can barely hear myself, so hopefully Gage caught my response. I'd better say it again. Clearing my throat, I nod. "That'd be nice."

"Yeah?" He nods. "Great."

We stare at each other for way too long. An awkward amount of time. Until he breaks the silence with a question. "Daisy, can I ask you something about that night?"

I know which night. "Sure."

He pulls out his notebook from his chest pocket and flips the pages around. "You said you saw the redhead when you came upstairs from getting your laundry. Is that right?"

"Yes."

"And you didn't see her enter Kara's apartment?"

Shaking my head, I repeat what I said before. "No."

"And when you went back into your apartment, you didn't hear anything? No conversations between the redhead and Kara?"

I shake my head again.

"Nothing later?"

"No."

"How can that be? You knew when Finch and I were in the apartment. You're very cognizant of what's happening in the hallway. Why not that night?"

It's a good question. One I answered, but I'll repeat it. "I put on my headphones when I got back into my apartment."

"Those prevent you from hearing anything?"

"They're noise canceling. I listen to them while I work."

"While you do research?"

"Yes."

"How long did you work? With the headphones on?"

I get why he's asking. I heard them say something about the time of death; it was between the time I saw the redhead and two or three hours after that. "I worked for a few hours. I tend to work late into the night."

"So did I wake you this morning?" He's sliding the notebook back into his pocket along with his pen. I guess we're done with the questioning portion of the morning.

"I was awake." I say it with a smile. "Barely."

"Sorry." I do believe Mr. Golden is blushing. "Since I've taken over the investigation—"

"You're in charge now?" I don't know why that surprises me. He's probably the best officer on the Ames police force.

"I am." More blushing, and it's adorable.

"Congratulations."

"Thanks." Clearing his throat, he continues. "I usually work nights, but now that I'm doing this, I've got to be in early."

"I get it."

"So, my apologies if I woke you."

If he only knew how much I'd like him to wake me up *every* morning…. "No worries. My sleep patterns are all over the place."

"Mine too." Gage chuckles, and I want to grab him by his collared shirt and drag him to my bed, but I can't. Not today. I've got too much to do.

His eyes move from me to somewhere behind me. "Wow, you've really cleared out the place."

I look back at my relatively sparse living room. "Yeah. I got rid of my mom's stuff." Most of it.

"It looks nice, Daisy."

And there it is again. My name. Holy hotness, my panties just melted.

"Thanks."

And we're back to the staring at each other thing. If I didn't need to be somewhere in less than an hour, I'd keep right on looking at this man with his blond hair and pretty smile. But I can't. "Well, I need to get going." I jerk my thumb backward. "I've got to shower and get out of here."

"Right." Gage runs his fingers through his wavy hair. My fingers itch. I want to do that for him. "I'll, uh, talk to you soon."

"Good luck with the investigation." Because the sooner he solves this thing, the sooner we can eat together.

Wow, did that sound as anticlimactic as I think it did?

"Thanks." Gage waves, turns, and walks down the hallway.

Shutting the door, I lean my back against it and sigh. "That man is going to be my undoing."

CHAPTER TWELVE

Gage

"That woman is something else." When she opened the door in that little tank top, I nearly passed out. Not only that, her hair was down and sort of messy from sleep, and her glasses were long gone. I was right. She's all curves and softness. "Damn." She might be the prettiest girl I've ever seen.

My phone vibrates in my pocket. Sliding it out, I see a message from another very pretty woman.

Quinn: We're back in Ames. Can we meet?

I've been expecting her call. According to Cooke Thompson, they were due back about now. Since Tayler's out on bail, I'm sure she wants an update. I just hope I can give her news she can live with.

Me: Sure. Let me see what my day looks like and I'll get back to you.
Quinn: Sounds good. Thanks, Gage.
Me: Talk to you later.

At the station, things are at a standstill. The team consists of me, the captain, Finch, and surprisingly, Dan Trumbull, who decided to make an appearance today. We brought in a veteran officer, Jane Bradshaw, as well. She specializes in the behavioral science or psychology part of this kind of crime. Trust me, she's good.

"So, typically what we call a crime of passion, I'd prefer to call an impulse murder because it's a sudden, strong impulse such as sudden rage rather than a premeditated crime."

That part of Jane's statement isn't a surprise. We're all familiar with that part of the definition. But what she said next piqued my interest. "We're all biologically predisposed to violence in certain situations."

I'm not sure I agree with that, necessarily, but she's the one with the psych degree.

"Our brains are wired for danger," she continues. "And when we sense danger, we use our defense mechanisms, which are often violent, for our own survival."

Okay, I can see that. But how does that relate to this murder? "So, our perpetrator felt as though they were in danger?" I hedge.

"Perhaps not physical or bodily danger. They may have felt something much more abstract. Our victim could have been threatening something else. Their livelihood, for example. Or threatening another person who they feel the need to protect."

"You're really broadening our pool of suspects," Dan grouses.

"Well, let me try to narrow this down for you." She leans forward in her seat in our conference room. "Statistically speaking, our perp is most likely male but we can't rule out a female. They're right-handed based on the blood splatter, though the height of the suspect is unclear, because it appears they swung the club more than once and from two different angles: one as the victim stood and the other as she was going down."

Finch makes a grunting noise.

"Yes, Finch?" Jane asks with a smirk.

"So, it could have been a man or a woman?"

She smirks. "Yep. Due to the choice of weapon, it could have been either." She narrows her eyes like she's angry. "A woman can be just as strong as a man, Finch."

"I know," he responds defensively. "I know."

"So, we know nothing." Finch says like it's nothing. "It could be a guy or a girl. They could be tall or short. Fat or thin?"

"Body weight..." Jane starts to respond but I hold up my hand.

"We don't know, right?" I look at Jane. "We're back to square one."

With a little sigh, Jane nods.

AFTER THE MEETING, IT'S DAN'S TURN TO TELL US WHAT HE'S learned from Kara Becker's social media. Leaning back in my chair, I wait for his report.

"She was a little bitch."

Wow, that's one way to open the conversation.

Dan hands us a packet—pages from her journal have been copied and stapled together. A second stack of papers lands on the table in front of me. "Those are screenshots of her Snappy-whatever account, but she mostly used Twipper."

Twipper? Apparently Dan's not up on the latest apps the kids are using.

"I've made notations and numbered some of the journal entries because they coincide with shit she posted." He sighs. "She was mean as a pit bull."

"Hey, man," Finch interjects. "Pit bulls are sweet."

With an eye roll, Dan changes his phrasing. "Okay. She was as mean as a snake with a toothache." He glares at Finch. "Better?"

Finch merely nods.

We're getting off track.

"Can we keep going, Dan?" I ask.

"I'd like to," he grumbles. "So, I've noted the entries with the same dates as the social media shit. If you look at the journal entry from June 22"—we all turn our pages—"she's writing about someone with the initials DF in the journal."

"Dylan Forrester," the captain interjects.

I take a minute to read her journal. In it, she goes into detail about Dylan's, um, prowess in bed—or lack thereof. From her details, he wasn't good.

"Yep." Dan nods. "Now, turn to the Twinker posting on the same day."

We all turn to the other packet. I flip pages until I get to the one dated June 22.

Kara @beautifulbecker

#speedkills Be warned, @dylanforrester is faster than a speeding bullet. Don't bother, ladies.

8:08 AM – Jun 22

Dan continues, "Now, look back at February 18."

We all flip through the pages. I go ahead and do the same with the social media pages.

I read both and say, "She's talking about someone named Bryant Falco."

Kara @beautifulbecker

#takingonefortheteam If any of you are interested in @bryfalco as a sexual partner, don't bother. #tinydick

"Harsh."

Ignoring the captain's remark, I ask, "Do we know who this Falco is?" As I look around the room, the only thing I see are heads shaking. "Let's find him and anyone else she targeted in this shit." As I flip through the pages, I glimpse a "Q" and a "u" and I instantly know it was about Quinn. I probably shouldn't read it, but I open the journal packet anyway.

What is the deal with Quinn Fat Maxwell? Everyone loves her. Why? She's stupid, plain, and her clothes are U-G-L-Y. I guess everyone likes to root for the loser. But not me. She's going down.

I note the date and search her social media for the same day.

Kara @beautifulbecker
    Hey, people—stop feeling sorry for the fat girls. Instead, encourage them to eat a damn carrot once in a while. #fatlivesdonotmatter

"Jesus," I mutter. "What a fucking bitch."

"Told ya," Dan says with a small chuckle. "We should check out all these people she slammed on here. I bet it pissed off quite a few."

"I bet you're right." Turning to Finch, I smile. "Guess what you get to do?"

"Already making a list of names to check out."

"Keep in mind this journal was only from the last year," Dan points out.

"She may have another one at home." Turning to Billings, I say, "Captain, we need to check out Kara's home. Will Mr. Becker let us search her bedroom?"

He nods. "I think so. I'll talk to him when he stops in later."

"Great." I look at Dan. "As soon as we get the thumbs-up, we should head out there."

Stuart, Iowa. "It's about two hours from here."

"No problem." Except for the four hours I'll have to be in a car with Dan.

∼

"THANKS FOR MEETING US, GAGE."

When I said I'd meet Quinn for coffee, I'd hoped she'd be alone, but I'm not sure that's ever going to happen again. I think she's attached at the hip to this guy.

"Mate." Cooke Thompson reaches out and shakes my hand over the table. "Thanks for taking the time."

"No problem. But I only have about thirty minutes." It turns out Kara's father was more than happy to let us check out her bedroom, so we're heading out to his place this afternoon. But I need to get a few things together before we take off.

"So, do you have any news?" Quinn's voice is tentative. "Tayler's going a little crazy, to be honest."

Cooke scoffs.

"We have a few leads—"

"Another suspect?" She suddenly sounds excited.

I don't want to give anything away since we really don't have anything solid. "We're checking out all leads."

She rolls her eyes. "Now you sound like you've got a cheat sheet of things to say when you're not supposed to tell anyone what's really going on."

She's right. "Look." I lean closer and lower my voice. "We're seriously checking out everyone." Hell, we even looked at the video footage of every person who came and went through the front door of Kara's building. The management has been nice enough to identify those who actually live in the building and those who don't. Two of our patrol officers have questioned the residents to no avail.

Quinn sighs dramatically. "Okay. I get it."

The urge to reach out and take hold of her hand is strong, but I keep my hands to myself. "We don't know enough just yet."

"But Tayler's not the killer." Quinn looks at me, then at Cooke.

"Mate, just drop the charges on Tayler so we can get back to our lives."

That statement irritates me. "Oh, I'm so sorry that this has upset your lives so much. I'll be sure to tell Mr. Becker how badly you want this to be over." I mean....

"No." Cooke shakes his head. "Apologies, mate. I didn't mean it that way. That's insensitive of me."

I nod because yeah, it was.

Cooke looks apologetic. "Just... the girls are beside themselves with worry, which makes me fret."

"I get it. I do. But you're just going to have to wait until we know more." Hell, we may never know who killed her, but hopefully we'll solve this thing.

"We get that, Gage." Quinn looks like she's about to cry. "This is all so...." A tear trickles down her pretty face, and I want to reach out and take it away from her, but the big English oaf gets to it first.

"Love," he says to her softly. "Gage is going to get the killer."

I nod because the need to make her stop crying is overwhelming. "I'm going to do my damn best, Quinn. I promise."

"I know." She sniffles. "It's just so bizarre." She pauses. Looking me in the eye, she blinks like she just realized something. "I think I'm lucky I was out of the country when it happened." She peers at me expectantly.

She *is* lucky, because if she'd been around here, she'd be my number one suspect. Well, maybe number two suspect. She had the motive. Kara's obsession with her would have made anyone snap.

Giving her a small smile, I have to agree. "I'm glad you weren't here too." As I stand to leave, I say, "I'll keep you posted."

"I know. Thank you, Gage."

Shit, she sounds defeated, and I hate it.

Looking at my watch, I wave as I head to the door. Turning one more time before I exit, I'm about to smile at Quinn when I see Cooke lean in and kiss my... and kiss Quinn. It's not a long kiss, but it looks like one that means something. I expect my heart to sink a little at the sight, but for some reason, I'm okay with it.

CHAPTER THIRTEEN

Daisy

As I unlock my apartment door, I'm singing to myself. I'm not a great singer, but I can carry a tune, and the one I just heard in my car is catchy. I can't get it out of my head. That is until I see who's made themselves at home in my living room.

"Dad." *What is he doing here?*

Placing my shopping bags on the floor next to the front door, I step into the living room and see a mess. A big mess that appears to be some of my papers, file folders, and a few notebooks. Not only that, but Mom's precious *Vogue* magazine is in shreds on the coffee table in front of him.

Why? Why is he like this?

"What are you wearing?" he says in that tone I hate. The judgmental one.

I look down at myself. "A dress." A cute green and yellow floral sundress. It's not my style, but I like it. It reminds me of something someone in one of my books would wear to a garden party. Do people still have garden parties?

"A bit cold to be wearing that flimsy thing, isn't it?"

I paired it with a jean jacket, so no, it's not that cold. I choose to ignore his comment. In his defense—which he doesn't deserve

—he's not used to seeing me in anything other than leggings and oversized sweatshirts. By his thin lips and glare, I'd say he doesn't like it.

I decide at that moment to ask my own question. "Dad, what's all this?" I point to the mess. As quickly as I can, I scan the things strewn about to see if I can determine what he's after.

"I'm just trying to figure out what you were doing today."

I blink, thinking. I need to remain calm and aloof, so I shrug. "Just running errands."

"Errands?" he asks, standing up from the sofa.

"Yes."

"What kind of errands did you need to take care of at First National Bank."

No. He. Didn't. "You followed me?"

He doesn't bother answering. "We don't bank at First National."

We? What he means is we have a joint account at Vista Credit Union. It's the account he deposits my rent money into along with the little bit of spending money he gives me.

"What were you doing at the bank, Daisy?" Dad's voice has gotten calm. Too calm.

The thing is, I've been prepared for something like this. I knew I'd have to have a backstory for some of the things I've done until I'm ready to make my final move. "I was there about a loan."

"A loan?" He takes two steps closer. "Why would *you* need a loan?"

"I wanted to buy a gaming computer." And those things are like four grand, so it makes sense that I'd need a loan.

"Why not go to Vista? We've been their customer for years."

"I wanted to do it on my own." That's a viable excuse, right?

Two steps closer. We're less than a foot apart now. "Why don't I believe you?"

Ugh, his voice is starting to sound a little creepy.

"Dad." I sigh, then roll my eyes for effect. "I'm twenty-three years old. It's time I—"

"No!" he shouts so loudly I jump. "It's not time. It's not time for you to do a goddamn thing."

"Dad, I—" I don't get any other words out.

"Don't." He inches closer. "Whatever you're up to, I'll find out. The bank president of First National is a friend of mine."

I want to tell him good luck with that, but I choose to remain silent.

"Does this have anything to do with your visitor this morning?"

Okay. That's too much. "What were you doing, hiding in the stairwell?" I laugh, but it comes out as more of a grunt. "He brought me back my plastic container. That's it."

"And you invited him over for dinner."

And that's enough of that. Now *I* step closer. We're nose to nose. Well, his nose to my forehead. I look up into his eyes and say what I've needed to say for years. "I'm only going to say this once, *Dad*." I grit my teeth. "If you don't back the fuck off, I won't finish your fucking book."

"And if you don't finish my fucking book, I won't give you your allowance."

I push up onto my tiptoes. "And if you don't give me my allowance, I've got a friend of my own at the *Ames Tribune*." That's no lie. Well, we used to be friends in high school, until I practically became a recluse.

"You wouldn't dare."

"Try me." Seriously. I want him to try me. I've been dying to go to the paper or to someone about him for years.

He suddenly takes a step back. "Fine." Running his hand through his perfectly coifed hair, he chuckles. "You surprise me, Daisy Fay." He turns and walks to my patio door. The one I haven't seen out of for years. The sunlight makes a big difference in this place. I no longer feel like I live in a cave.

While I'm at it, I add, "Back off about my personal life."

So suddenly it startles me, Dad's head whips back until his glaring eyes meet mine. "Do not test me on that. No visitors. No dates. And especially no cops."

"Why the hell not?"

"Because cops snoop."

"Nobody will find out about our deal unless I'm the one who shares it."

Dad's voice is low and rumbly. "You'd better not." He means "or else."

I shrug. "That's up to you, old man."

I guess calling him "old man" is funny because he laughs as he walks past me, bumping me with his shoulder like some punk-ass. At my door, he looks back at me as he reaches for the knob. "I'm going to call my friend at that bank."

"Do whatever you need to do." Because he won't find out shit. The asshole.

CHAPTER FOURTEEN

Gage

The ride to Stuart, Iowa, has ended up being a working drive. Finch is driving because the captain thought the experience would be good for the rookie. I guess he's right. So while Finch drives, Trumbull has taken shotgun. That left me with the back seat. I was a little irritated by that at first, but I've used the extra space to spread out some of my notes and a copy of the file on Kara Becker's murder.

With everything in front of me and two other brains in the car, we've worked through some of the questions I've had rolling around in my head. Things like the surveillance video taken at Social Apartments. "It shows Tayler Sorenson arriving at the time she said and leaving approximately eighteen minutes later."

"Still time enough to kill Becker," grumbles Dan.

"Yeah, but there's nothing odd about her demeanor as she leaves. If you'd just murdered someone, wouldn't you behave differently?" I know I would. "Plus, there doesn't appear to be any blood on her clothing, and she's wearing the same thing she had on when she got there."

"But she's wearing dark jeans and a dark shirt. Blood would

have been hard to spot, especially since the video was grainy, at best." Dan makes a good point.

"Okay. But what about the garage entrance?" I ask, hoping one of them has some new information on that. At Social, there are parking spaces beneath the building that some residents choose to rent. The fees are added to the cost of the rent, so I've got a list of the residents who have a spot. Kara Becker had one, for example. Daisy is another. For those people, there's a service elevator that takes them up from the underground parking to their floor. "Do we know when we're going to get the elevator footage yet?"

From the corner of my eye, I see Dan nodding. "Captain said we should get that today or tomorrow."

"Nothing from the parking garage itself?"

"I checked with management, and they said that camera is out of order." Finch is proving to be pretty good at this stuff.

"Jesus," I mutter. That's dangerous. Assaults happen all the time in dark, dank places like that. I immediately think of Daisy. Not only that, I'm sure other women have spaces down there, and I'd bet they're expecting it to be safe for them, but if the security camera doesn't work, that's dangerous.

"Finch," I snap.

"Yeah?"

"Call their management *today* and tell them if they don't get that repaired this week, I'm calling Ames Inspection Division. Maybe a hefty fine is what they need to get that shit done."

"Yes, sir." Surprisingly, Finch doesn't sound like a smartass when he says that.

"Thanks." I pick up the photocopied journal that Dan created. "Becker seems to have quite a few comments about the guys she sleeps with in here."

"She has a rating system," Dan explains.

I read about another guy we should check out. "Evan Parker got a C+."

"Hey. That's as good as an A. Every other guy seems to score a D or lower in that book."

"That's rough," Finch grumbles.

Dan looks out his window. "And really shitty. To judge a guy like that."

"Guys do that kind of shit all the time," Finch adds. "The dudes in my frat had contests."

"You were in a frat?" That says a lot about this guy. Frat guys are a pain in the ass.

He nods. "For a year, but then I quit. Guys were pricks."

Alrighty then. I guess I was wrong about Finch. Again.

I leaf through the pages once more.

"So, she used initials here for some of the people. DF, which I'm going to assume is Dylan Forrester again."

"She didn't have much good to say about him. She gave him a D-minus in the sack. And as we read from her social media post, the guy was quick." Dan chuckles. "Poor girl."

"And then there's Bryant Falco."

"He's mentioned several times, along with Quinn Maxwell." Dan reaches back and takes the packet from my hand. "Here. Let me find it."

"With Quinn?" I pick up my phone. "Hang on." Without a thought, I type out a message to Quinn.

Me: Do you know someone named Bryant Falco?

Seconds later, I get a response.

Quinn: He was a guy I used to like. A friend. Why?
Me: Did he know Kara Becker?
Quinn: Yes. They dated for a while.
Me: You have his number?
Quinn: Yeah. It's been a while since I've used it, but I'll

send you what I've got. You don't think Bryant killed her, do you?

Me: Just part of the investigation. His name came up. We need to check out every avenue.

Quinn: I get it.

A moment later, I receive his number.

Me: Thanks.

Quinn: Anytime.

Pulling out my notebook, I flip the pages back until I've got my notes from my conversation with the women from Beedle Drive. Thumbing through, I get to the part where they reference a guy who Kara dated. The one who was a friend of Quinn's. Susanna called him "Bradley," and Robbi thought it was "Braxton." I'd bet my badge they meant Bryant Falco.

Jotting down his name and number in my notebook, I tell the guys, "Got his number. Finch. Call him. We definitely need to bring him in for a chat."

"I'll get him in there." Finch sounds confident, which is good. We need confidence right now because the more we work, the more suspects we seem to be gathering.

Reading through Kara's journal again, I tell them, "She gave Falco an F."

Poor bastard.

Reading on, I see two initials I've seen before. Starting over, I run through the first page to my current spot for something that indicates who it is. "Who's DG?"

Dan turns to look at me. "That, I couldn't figure out. The initials were mentioned several times starting last year—October or November, I think—but no clues as to who he or she is."

I flip through several more journal pages. "Those letters are in here a number of times. Let's keep an eye out for them as we search her room."

"Agreed." Finch says from the driver's seat.

"So, what else are we looking for today?" asks Finch.

That's a good question. "I'd say anything that relates to her life in Ames."

"Are we talking to the father today?"

Dan takes this one. "Captain said kid gloves around the dad. We can ask, and if he wants to answer questions, he can."

So that's what we'll do.

CHAPTER FIFTEEN

Daisy

As soon as my dad is gone, I take a moment to gather myself. No matter how cool and collected I seemed, inside I was shaking like a leaf. Based on the things he ransacked from my files and drawers, I can see he didn't find anything that would indicate I was up to no good. And I *am* up to no good—as far as my father's concerned. No, I keep anything that would incriminate myself in another location. One he doesn't have access to, and he never will. It's taken me six years to put my plan into action, and this is it. As soon as that damn book is done, *so am I*.

CHAPTER SIXTEEN

Gage

"Well, how'd you fellas do?" Captain Billings asks us as soon as we walk back into the police station.

"We didn't find much," mumbles Dan. "And her father knew less about his kid than we do."

"Now that's not fair." I glare at Dan. Then, looking over at the captain, I say, "He's still really shaken by her death."

"I can see that." The captain has three kids himself. Hell, even if Kara had been my child, I'd feel the same as Becker, and that's knowing the kind of person she was. She was still his only child. Well, I guess there was another one, but she died very young.

Setting a file box down on my desk, I explain, "We were given permission to bring back her school papers, notebooks, and anything from her life in Ames that we thought could give us some clues as to what she was up to. Finch inventoried everything, and we had Mr. Becker sign off on it."

"Excellent." He beams at Finch like a proud father. I'd like to snicker, but that's unprofessional. I'll wait until I get home.

The three of us make a couple trips down to the car to bring up the items we took from Kara's bedroom. It's doubtful we'll find anything worthwhile in this mess, but we've got to try.

"I guess we're gonna be spending the next few days in the office," I say glumly. I hate the desk part of this job. I'd prefer to be moving. But this is as much a part of an investigation as anything.

I look at the clock. "It's getting late." Plus, I'm fucking starving. "Why don't we get a fresh start in the morning?"

"I agree," says Finch. "I need to eat and get home to my girl."

Dan's face says everything. He doesn't have a girl to get home to. Not anymore. "I'm gonna order in some food and get started. You two head home. I need some alone time. Spending eight fucking hours with you two in one day is more than I can take."

I don't think he really feels that way. I suspect it's his way of letting us get out of here. But he's right. I've had enough male bonding to last me a while. "I'll be here first thing to pick up where you left off."

"Sounds good."

On the way out, Finch catches up to me. "I think he just doesn't want to go home."

I nod. What else can I say to that? "See you at seven?" I ask with an arched brow.

"Sure. I'll be here," he practically chirps.

I'm a little surprised by how eager he sounds.

You know, I think I may have been wrong about Lance Finch.

AT HOME, I SHOWER AND CHANGE INTO A PAIR OF SWEATS AND a tee. My food should be delivered any minute, and I can't wait. My stomach has been growling for a couple of hours now. Tonight, I opted for some pizza from Great Plains Sauce and Dough Company. I asked for extra honey for my whole wheat crust. Just the thought of it makes my stomach growl in anticipation.

Pulling out my one and only TV tray, I grab a beer and

settle onto my sofa. My cat, Pepper Anderson, takes the opportunity to jump up for a little scratch behind her ear. She loves when I do that. Leaning back, I sip my beer and pet the cat. She must like it because she crawls onto my lap, curls up into a ball, and begins purring. No doubt she's as tired as I am with my new schedule. We had sort of an ideal thing going since we're both essentially nocturnal, but now that I'm working days, things are a little screwed up. I know I'm exhausted, so maybe she is too.

"You miss me today, Pep?" Of course she doesn't respond. I sigh and close my eyes. I'm home, I'm comfortable, and my stomach is about to be filled to the brim with pizza. What's better than that?

When the doorbell rings, I practically launch off the couch, startling the cat and causing her to jump off my lap and skitter out of the room. *Food!* As soon as I open the door, I can already smell the scent of sauce and cheese. Since I paid online, I take the pizza and hand the delivery guy a few bucks. "Thanks."

"No problem-o, dude."

Shutting the door, I don't bother with plates or napkins or silverware. "It's just me and you," I say to the pizza box. Placing it on the tray, I pop open the box. Just as I'm reaching for my first slice, my phone rings.

"No," I whine.

I make eye contact with what would have been my first slice, then glance at the phone. I see the name and forget the pizza.

"Daisy. What's wrong?"

Yes, I've added her to my contacts.

"Oh, um." She sounds hesitant. "I'm sorry to call you so late, but...,"

"But what? Is everything okay?"

"Yes. Well, no."

Jesus. I need her to spit it out. "Are you in danger?"

"Well, no. I don't think so."

I'm this close to pulling my hair out. "Tell me what you need."
Now, please.

"It's just... I remembered something."

"Remembered something?"

"About that night."

The night Kara was murdered. "Okay. What'd you remember."

"Well, it was earlier, you know, when I went to put my clothes in the wash."

There's a long pause. "Uh-huh."

"I was searching for coins because those machines eat money."

I remain silent.

"Anyway, when I was heading down, I saw Kara. She must've just been getting home."

"What time was this?"

"I'd say around eight or so."

"And was there something significant about seeing Kara?"

"Well, no." She hesitates. "Well, sort of. She was all dressed up, you know, like she was going to a job interview or something."

Interesting. Where would she have been going at that time dressed up?

"That's not it, though. It was the thing she was holding."

"Which was?"

"A big pink envelope."

"Pink?"

"Yeah, like hot pink... magenta."

I do my best to remember the list of items we took from her apartment. No pink envelope that I recall.

"And you said big? Like nine by twelve?"

"Yeah, like one of those bigger ones that holds a full sheet of paper."

"Okay. That's good information."

"It is?" She sounds sincerely surprised.

"It is. I'll check tomorrow to see if we recovered a large pink envelope. You may have cracked this case wide open." I chuckle.

"Oh." Silence, then, "You're teasing me." Her voice changes in that instant to something that sounds distinctly hurt.

"No. I mean it. It's a line from every old cop show ever made. I've always wanted to say it." But now I don't plan to say it ever again.

"Oh." She sounds unsure. "Okay. Well, thanks. Good night."

"Wait," I say too loudly. "I really mean it. That's very helpful, and it could be a key to all of this."

"Really?"

"Really... Daisy." I almost called her sweetheart. Thank god I didn't. That'd be very inappropriate. "Any and all information you can give me, us, will be helpful."

She sighs and I hold my breath, waiting for her words. "No. I get it. I'm glad I could help."

Several seconds tick by before she says, "Well, I'd better go."

"Listen... I just got a pizza delivered." *Oh shit. What am I doing?*

"Crap. I'm sorry. Why didn't you say anything? I just—"

"No, I mean... do you want to come over?" *Seriously, what the ever-loving hell am I doing?*

"But you said—"

"I know what I said. There's nothing wrong with us being friends." Shit. I just friend-zoned her.

"Right. Friends."

I wait for her to tell me she has other plans when she finally speaks. "What kind of pizza?"

My heart sort of flutters a little in my chest at her question. Is that weird? Should my heart flutter? Maybe I should get that checked out. "Great Plains. The Herbivore's Delight on whole wheat, but I added pepperoni."

Her laugh makes me smile. "You got a vegetarian pizza with meat?"

"I did. It's the best."

"Actually, it sounds delicious. Are you sure you have enough?"

"How much are you gonna eat?" I laugh. "I bought a large. I even got extra honey."

"Oh, wow. I love dipping the crust in the honey."

Me too. "So, are you in?"

"I'm in. This is my cell, so text me your address. I'll be over in... well, soon."

"Great."

We hang up, and I send her my address. If she leaves right now, it'll take her fifteen to twenty minutes to get here. That gives me a little time to tidy up my place and change into jeans and a shirt that doesn't have holes in the armpits.

CHAPTER SEVENTEEN

Daisy

What am I doing? I can't believe I'm about to step onto Gage Golden's front porch.

I take a moment to look at his little bungalow. Actually, the entire neighborhood is adorable. The streetlights look like old-time gas lamps that are bright enough for me to see what his place looks like. It's cute and very neat. The grass is cut, and there are pretty flowers in beds all around the porch that extends the entire length of the front of the house. Taking two steps up, I find myself on a porch that's the perfect spot for a swing.

"Oh God." I attempt to swallow my nerves down. "I can't believe I'm about to knock on Gage Golden's front door." His *yellow* front door. If I told you I've always wanted a yellow front door, would you think I was nuts?

Just as I'm about to knock, his door opens wide, and I nearly choke. Gage in a police uniform is a sight to behold, but in a pair of jeans and a snug tee and bare feet? Well, I may just die from happiness on the spot. It's my favorite look by far. He's casual while still being rugged and sexy as hell.

"Damn." I sort of mumble the word, but I think he heard me.

"I could say the same."

I look down at the dress I've been wearing all day. The green and yellow floral one. "Oh, this old thing?" I giggle at my stupidity. He's not the only one who can reference old shows.

"You look really nice."

"Thanks."

We stand there, me still on his front porch, him in his doorway, until I make a slight motion with my hand.

"Oh, shit." He chuckles as he moves out of the doorway. "Come in. Please."

Following him in, I smile when I see the inside of this house. Everything looks updated with fresh paint and refinished floors, but there's still the essence of male all around thanks to the oversized black leather sectional sofa and matching chair. They're so large, they pretty much take up the entire space.

The room is open to the kitchen, which looks as though it's been updated with some kind of stone counters. Marble or granite, Though I can't be sure. "I like your place."

"Yeah?" He smiles proudly. "I've been working on it."

"By yourself?"

"Mostly." Running a hand through his blond waves, he adds, "But there are things that just aren't in my wheelhouse."

"Like?"

"Electrical and plumbing. I hired people to do those things."

"Smart. Flood and fire are two of the worst things that can happen to a home."

Even though I was serious, he must find it hilarious because he throws his head back and laughs. I don't hate it. Gage Golden laughing, or with any kind of smile, is magnificent.

When he stops laughing, he points to his couch. "Have a seat. I kept the pizza warm in the oven. Let me grab it." Turning to head into the kitchen, he asks, "What would you like to drink? I've got beer, water, and lemon-lime soda."

"Water, please."

"Got it."

I sit on the sofa and sink in, wiggling until my spine meets with the back. It's so deep my feet are now sticking straight out in front of me. See what I mean? His sofa his huge. It's so big there's no room for a dining table in this space, apparently.

While I wait for him to return from the kitchen, I fiddle with the bottom of my dress—and scream.

From out of nowhere, a cat has jumped onto my lap.

"What's wrong?" Gage shouts as he races from the kitchen.

"Y-You've g-got a cat?" I hate cats. Well, correction. I'm scared of cats. There's a difference. A slight one.

"Pepper. *Get down*." Gage places a hand on the feline's body and pushes her off my lap. Kneeling in front of me, he looks up at me with worry in his eyes. "Are you okay? I should have warned you about the cat."

Shaking my head, I reach out and touch his arm. "No. I'm sorry I panicked. Cats and me...." How do I say it? "Cat's don't usually like me."

"Pepper must've liked you to come to you." He smiles. "She's finicky about who she lets pet her."

"Really?" If that's the case, maybe I could try again. "Her name's Pepper?" It's a strange name for a yellow cat.

"My mom named her Pepper Anderson."

I laugh. "She's got a last name?"

"Yeah." He runs his fingers through his hair. "Pepper Anderson was the name of a character in a show called *Police Woman* back in the 70s, I think. It was one of her favorite shows, and since I'm a cop...."

"Your mom named her?"

"My mom gave her to me as a housewarming gift." He rolls his eyes. "Who gives cats as gifts?"

I laugh again. "Your mom must be funny."

"She is." He looks me in the eye. "You going to be okay with Pepper here?"

"Oh. Yeah." I wave off his question. "She just startled me."

"Okay," he says hesitantly. "If you feel scared at all, let me know. I can put her in my bedroom and shut the door."

"No. Don't. This is her house too."

"If you're sure?" He pushes himself up to stand.

"I'm sure." I'm not so sure, but I need to try. For Gage.

I watch him return to the kitchen. He's back in no time. "Here we are." He brings two plates, forks, napkins, and a glass of water. They're all balanced precariously on top of a box labeled with the restaurant known for their crust.

"Mm." I can't help making that noise. This pizza is amazing. "Smells good."

He places the box with everything on top onto the coffee table before handing me my water. I take a sip and watch him work. Next, I'm given a plate with two slices of pizza along with a napkin and fork. "Here." He pushes over a TV tray circa 1965. It's covered in the famous boomerang pattern I remember seeing on my grandmother's dining table.

I set my plate on the tray. "Thank you." Looking around the room, I expect to see another tray, but it looks as though he only has one. Why does that make me smile? Heck, it makes me giddy. Because if he had more than one, he'd have two, and I'd be wondering who the other one was for. But just to be sure. "Is this your only tray? Because I don't need one."

"No worries." He smiles. "I'm used to sitting like this." I watch him as he sits about two feet from me. He sets his beer between his legs and his plate on top of that, so it rests on his thighs. "Sorry. No dining room."

"No." I smile at him. A sincere one. "This is how I do it at home too." Picking up one of my pizza slices, I close my eyes for my first bite. I want to savor it. "Oh Gob," I say with my mouth full of yummy pizza. "So goob."

I open my eyes and blush when I see Gage watching me. To say his gaze is intense is an understatement. He quickly shakes his head and looks down at his food. "I'm starving." I watch as he devours two slices in the time I've barely finished one. "You were hungry. Busy day?"

"Yeah. We drove out to Stuart, Iowa."

"Stuart? Where's that?"

"It's a couple of hours from here. West of Des Moines."

"Why?" I assume it's for the investigation.

"Kara's hometown."

"Oh." I look down at my plate as a sense of sadness washes over me. "I feel for her family."

"Yeah. Her dad's taken it pretty hard."

"And her mom?"

"Out of the picture."

"I get that. I don't think my father would care if something happened to me, though." Except he'd be without his writer. He'll realize that's going to be a reality soon enough.

I feel Gage's hand touch mine, and a shiver runs up my arm. "Don't say that. I'm sure he'd be devastated."

I snort. "Believe me, Dr. Dorian Gray Buchanan only cares about himself."

He squeezes my arm a little. "I'm sorry, Daisy."

My goodness, the sound of his voice is so sweet, so sincere.

"Don't worry. I'm used to it. Besides"—I smile—"I'm not going to be doing his research for much longer."

"Oh?" He eats another slice of pizza in record time. Where the hell does he store the stuff? His body looks like he treats it like a temple. "What will you do when you're finished with that?"

"I've got something else lined up."

"Is it, um, here in Ames?"

"For now." I nod and reach out to get another piece of pizza. This will be my third and last. I'm already stuffed to the gills, but I don't get pizza very often. I feel like I need to indulge.

"Here." He hands me the honey. "For the crust."

"Oh, I forgot." Damn. Now I'll be so full, I'll have to waddle out of here.

"So, this new job…," he asks tentatively.

"It'll be remote, so I can work from anywhere."

"Oh." He smiles. "Good."

Hell yes. He said "good."

I'M NOT SURE WHAT TO DO AFTER WE'VE FINISHED DINNER, SO I ask, "Can I help you clean up?" I know, it's only two plates and a pizza box, but it's impolite not to offer.

"Nah. I've got it."

Should I leave?

"Want to watch a movie or something?"

Thank goodness he brought it up.

Not wanting to lose this thread, I say, "Sure. Do you have any of the subscription channels? You know, like Netflix?" *Ooh, Netflix and chill.*

"No. I'm not here enough. I've got a bunch of DVDs in that cupboard next to the television. Go ahead and pick something out while I start up the dishwasher."

Opening the cupboard door, I'm not sure what I expect to see. Certainly not this. "You have every Harry Potter movie?"

"Yeah. I read all the books as they were released, so I had to see the movies. My family sent those over to me on the base while I was overseas."

Wait one second…. "You were in the service?"

"I was. Four years."

"Which branch?"

"Army. MP. Military police."

I guess it makes sense that's he's a cop now.

When he steps back into his living room, he's holding a fresh glass of water for me. "You sure you don't want a beer?" he asks.

"No. I'm driving. And Ames cops are hard-core."

He laughs again, like he did before. "You're right. They can be assholes."

"I've heard." I roll my eyes, then smile. Reaching in, I grasp my choice. "Let's watch the first Harry Potter."

"Sounds good." Taking it from me, he sets the movie up while I settle in on the sofa again.

When the opening credits start to roll, Gage steps backward, then turns. I had hopes of him sitting next to me on this sofa—you know, extra close with his hand on my thigh—but that's not going to happen if he's sitting in the chair.

Damn it.

CHAPTER EIGHTEEN

Gage

I *knew* if I sat next to her on my extra comfortable couch, I'd have wanted to get close to her. Touch her. Maybe even kiss her. But I can't, so I do the right thing and take the chair.

Damn it, this *sucks*, because I'm having such a great time with her. I don't remember the last time I felt this comfortable around a woman. There's an ease about her that I can't quite figure out, even though her life seems sort of sad and complicated—*she's* not. She's bright and happy and, like I said, easy.

Well, not easy in *that* sense, at least not that I know of, but comfortable. I'm not saying any of this right.

Comfortable, Gage? Jesus, she's not a blanket.

Clearing my throat, I ask her, "Have you read the books?"

"Oh yeah. Multiple times."

"And have you seen the movies?"

"I have. They aren't as good as the books, but I've seen them so many times now, they work."

"Agreed."

We both turn to watch the opening scene unfold. "God, I remember seeing this in the theater and holding my breath at this exact scene. It's magical."

I chuckle at her words. "It *is* magical."

"Smartass," she says, leaning over the arm of my sofa in an attempt to slap my arm.

I beat her to it, though. When she's about to make contact, I reach out and grasp her hand. When that happens, both of us freeze. She's staring at our clasped hands just like I am. Without thinking, I intertwine my fingers with hers, and I'm not sure how to describe the feeling other than to say it feels right. Very, very right.

Thankfully, she doesn't pull away. Instead, our joined hands rest on the arm of my chair for a good long time.

"Thanks," Daisy says with a shy smile. "I had a good time tonight."

"Me too." We're standing on my front porch now. The temperature dropped quite a bit since she arrived, so now she has her arms wrapped around herself. She's shivering.

"Hang on." I run back inside to my bedroom. Opening a dresser drawer, I pull out the sweatshirt on top. It's an old army one, gray and a little worse for wear. Rushing back out to the porch, I hand it to her. "Here. Put this on."

"Oh, no...," she says hesitantly.

"No. Please. It's too cold. Your dress is...." What? Flimsy? It looks like the fabric is light, and there aren't any sleeves.

Reaching out, she takes it. "I'll get it back to you."

"No worries." It is one of my favorites, but I can get another one.

"Thanks." She smiles.

I watch as she slips it over her head and then down. The bottom of it falls past her hips, and the arms swallow up her hands. She's adorable.

She scrunches up the sleeves, revealing her hands once again. I feel a hand on my shoulder and warm lips on my cheek. "Thanks," she says as she turns to leave.

"Text me when you get home."

"Okay," she agrees but doesn't look back.

"Drive safe."

This time she does. She laughs as she says, "Okay, Gage."

Damn. I don't want her to go, but it's the right thing to do. "Night."

"Night."

CHAPTER NINETEEN

Daisy

The minute I pull into my spot in the parking lot, I reach for my phone.

Me: Home.

I wait for his response. Actually, I'm holding my breath. Weird, right? I don't have to wait long.

Gage: Good. Had fun tonight.

Yeah, I should be cool and wait to respond, but why?

Me: Me too.
Gage: We should do it again. Watch the second one.
Me: I'd love to.
Gage: We could get food from...
Gage: What's your favorite restaurant in Ames?

That's a tough one. I have to think about it.

Me: Well, don't judge, but I love Blaze Pizza.

It's a chain restaurant, but I love their crust made crispy by the open-flame oven. Dang, I'm getting hungry just thinking about it.

Gage: Never been. Can't wait to try it.

I don't know what to say to that, so the smiley face will have to do.

Me: :)
Me: Night, Gage.
Gage: Night, Daisy.

Stepping out of my car, I've got a stupid grin on my face. It can't be helped. Unfortunately, that grin only lasts until I get to my apartment. It's there the smile drops because there's something taped to my door. An envelope. Moving closer, I see my name scribbled on the front in handwriting I recognize. Dad's. Grasping it, I carefully pull it away from the door so paint doesn't come off.

While I'd like to tear it open and read it now, I know I need to wait until I get inside. With key in hand, I open my door and step into my apartment. The sense something isn't right is immediate. Well, I guess I suspected something the minute I spotted the envelope. Moving past my kitchen, I freeze. "That fucker."

Yanking my phone from my pocket, I don't bother with the letter.

Me: Where's my computer?

He must've been waiting because he responds right away.

Daddy Dearest: In your old bedroom. With your clothing and the rest of your things. Didn't you read my note, honey?

"Honey" my ass.

Stomping into my bedroom, I see my bed has been stripped of all sheets, pillows, and blankets. No matter, I've got another set. Back in the hallway, I open the cupboard where I keep towels, sheets, blankets, and so on and growl. "That motherfucker." Everything's gone.

Well, the couch is still here. And the chair, coffee table, and my one stool. Also, the pictures on the wall and doodads on my shelf above the television are still in the same places.

I spend the next ten minutes looking through my closet, the bathroom, and the kitchen. He took everything I use every day, from my clothes to my toothbrush. It's all gone. The furniture's still here but I suppose he didn't have time for that.

Picking up the envelope, I tear it open and pull out the note.

Dear Daisy,

I can't believe I've been remiss. I should have insisted you move home the minute I heard about the incident across the hall from my apartment.

God, why does he always have to say it like that—"*my* apartment"? I read on.

It's too dangerous for you to remain, so I've taken the liberty of moving your necessities back home. Everything is set up in your bedroom. All you need to do is bring yourself. See you soon.

Love, Dad.

No. Fucking. Way.

With both hands, I rub my face up and down. I'm tired. It's late. And I'm *done*.

Flopping back onto my bed, I'm thankful Gage lent me his sweatshirt; otherwise, all I'd have to wear is this dress. Staring at the ceiling, I see a spider skitter across above me. I watch to make sure it doesn't stop above me and slither down a piece of web. Or maybe it's poisonous and he or she could go ahead and end this bullshit for me.

That could work.

No. I'm not suicidal. On the contrary. For the first time in a long time, I feel overwhelmingly strong. Like I'm ready for battle.

With a sigh—and the assurance the spider is gone—I roll over to my side. I've got to think. I mean, when did he plan all of this? It had to be today. Not only that, how'd he know I was gone tonight?

Suddenly, my body feels cold. The realization hits me like a Mack truck. I know how he knows—*the prick's been monitoring me*.

Sitting up, I look around my bedroom and shake my head. "No." No way he'd have a camera in my bedroom. Right?

Sliding out of bed, I walk into the living room and stop in the middle. Turning slowly in my spot, I scan the room, looking for anything that'd hide or obscure a camera. I know they're small now because I researched them for other reasons.

Never mind. Trust me. I know they're small.

I rotate around two times, looking at everything that remains after my father ransacked my place. It's then I see the perfect location for a camera. In the far corner of the living room, above the television, is a small shelf. On it I've got a few collectable items from trips we took when I was young. Back when we were a family. There's a snow globe from the Grand Canyon, various postcards, a keychain from a trip to Disney, a shot glass from Mount Rushmore, and the last item—from the time we went to a Chicago Cubs game—a bobblehead doll of Cubby Bear.

Moving slowly like I'm about to pounce on a rattler, I reach the shelf and stare up at Cubby Bear. Leaning as close as I can, it's then I spot it. Cubby Bear's eyes aren't the same. One is painted a matte black, but the other? It's shiny like glass. Reaching up, I take the toy in hand and pull the head away from the body, making the spring inside stretch. And there it is: several wires all attached to a tiny battery pack. Instead of ripping it from the head like I want to, I hold Cubby Bear out. Using my middle finger, I raise it slowly so he can see what I've discovered and to say "Fuck. You."

Now I reach in and yank out the wires. With those in one hand, I march into the kitchen and open drawers until I find the scissors, which I use to cut the wires up into tiny pieces. Tossing away the wires *and* Cubby Bear, I make my way back into my bedroom. Exhausted, I lie down, wrapping Gage's sweatshirt around me for warmth. And I cry.

CHAPTER TWENTY

Gage

I'm at the station before seven. When I walk in, I'm shocked to see Dan here. "Have you been at it all night?" God, I hope not. I'd feel like shit if he stayed while I had dinner with a pretty girl and then slept like a log.

"I left about two. Slept for a few hours, then came back." He pushes several items in front of me. "I think I've got something. Look—"

Just as he starts to speak, Finch steps in with a cup of coffee. Damn, I could use a cup right now. "Hey," he says, his voice sounding sleepy. "Sorry I'm late."

I look at the clock and see it's 7:01 a.m.

"No sweat." I nod to Dan. "He thinks he's found something."

"I don't know if it has anything to do with anything, but I thought it was worth a looksee," Dan explains.

Staring down at what looks to be report cards, I ask, "What are we looking at?"

"These are from last year." He points to the first page. "Fall term. Midterm grades." I look at the page he's referring to and read through her list of classes. She was enrolled in Math 140, Biology 201, Art History 280, and English 228.

I'm not sure which courses the numbers represent, but as I'm about to pull my phone out to check, Finch has beat me to it. Reading from his own phone, he says, "Math 140 is Algebra."

"Okay."

"Biology 201." He pauses. "Intro to Environmental Issues."

"Art History 280 is pretty self-explanatory," I say.

Finch nods. "English 228 is...." He nods after a beat. "Got it. Survey of American Lit since 1865."

Now that we know the courses, I look at her midterm grades. She had A's in both her art history and biology classes. In math, a C-. But the midterm grade for English? "She had an F in the American lit class."

"Yep, an F," repeats Dan. "Now look at this." He pulls out the second sheet. "Her final grades for fall."

"Wow. She really turned it around in English," Finch says with a nod.

I look at the sheet. Finch may be right. She got her shit together and raised her grade from an F to an A. It can happen.

"Uh-huh," Dan mumbles. "Check this out." He grabs the third sheet. "Her spring schedule."

I read through the list and see a sociology class, two education classes, a gym class, and another English course.

Before I can ask a question, Dan says, "I looked it up. English 362 was taught by the same professor as the English class she nearly flunked in the fall."

I look at Dan, then down at the papers. "And?"

"Well, if that were me," Finch says, pointing at her spring schedule, "and I struggled or had to work extra hard to pass the last English class, I don't think I'd take another one. At the very least, I'd take it with another professor."

"Do we have the grades for spring?"

Dan shakes his head. "Not in this stuff."

"Was there anything from her apartment?"

"We weren't looking for that," Finch says, stepping away from the table.

"We can try the registrar's office," Dan suggests as Finch grabs one of the boxes of papers from Kara's apartment and sets it in front of me. He does the same two more times until we each have a box to sort through.

"Probably need a subpoena," I mumble, reaching into the box to take a stack of papers. "Let's look through these and go from there."

With each of us sorting through her papers in silence, I can't help getting the feeling Dan was right and we're on to something.

After about forty minutes and two cups of terrible Ames PD coffee, Finch announces, "Got it."

Dan and I move in until we're looking over Finch's shoulder as he points. "Spring midterms."

Again, she does okay in her other classes, getting As and Bs, but English, another F.

"Did you find the final grades?" I ask Finch.

"Yep." He slaps down the second page. "She ended up with an A in English 362: Studies in 19th-Century American Lit."

We stare at the pages for several minutes. My mind is whirring.

"I'm still not sure why this is significant," Finch says. It's a good question.

"It may not be." Dan shrugs.

He's right. This could be a whole lot of nothing.

"You mentioned they were taught by the same person? Who was that?" I'm afraid I already know the answer to this question.

Dan moves some things around on the table until he finds what he's looking for. "Dr. D. Buchanan."

Shit. Instead of saying something I may regret, I say, "How 'bout the footage from the elevator in Kara's building?"

Finch begins to carefully place papers back into his box.

"Nothing yet." He looks over at me. "And Social Apartments' management promised to get the garage camera repaired today."

"Follow up with that today, will you?"

"Sure thing."

"What about Falco?"

Finch turns to face me and Dan. "Left a message."

"Okay. Keep on him. Call again until you get him."

"We could go to his place," he suggests. "I found an address for him."

"Good job, Finch." I nod. "Yeah. Let's try this afternoon."

Standing from my spot at the conference table, I turn to leave.

"Hey, Golden?"

Looking back at Finch, I wait.

"Isn't that girl... the one who made the cookies... isn't her last name Buchanan?"

"Yes."

"She any relation to that professor?"

"She may be." She is. I just need a minute before I relay that information to the team. "Let me use the john, and I'll check my notes when I get back."

"Cool." Finch smiles proudly. As he should. He's smart. He'll make a great cop in time.

CHAPTER TWENTY-ONE

Daisy

When a knock sounds on my front door, I'm startled awake. Looking around my room, I do my best to remember what day it is and why I'm so damn cold. The sight of my bed with no sheets, blankets, or pillows reminds me. I should have turned on the furnace last night, but I had other things on my mind.

The knocking redirects my attention to the front door. Sliding off the bed, I don't even bother looking in the mirror. I know I look like shit and that my hair probably resembles something close to a rat's nest, but I don't care.

Without looking through the peephole, I wrench the door open and stare at the man of my dreams and that other guy. The one who loved my cookies. "Oh." I do my best to get my hair under control, but it's no use. "Morning."

"It's afternoon, ma'am," the other guy deadpans.

"Rough night," I mumble. Turning, I walk back into my place, leaving the door open wide and hoping they just take the hint and follow me inside. I've got no energy to be courteous this morning —er, afternoon.

"You okay, Miss Buchanan?" Gage asks.

Miss Buchanan? Since when...? Flopping onto my couch, I tug on the sweatshirt he lent me last night. "What's going on?" Because this seems very official.

"Mind if we ask you a few more questions?" the other guy asks.

"No, I don't mind." I wish it were just me and Gage, but like I said, this seems super official.

I watch as Gage nods to the other guy. Since the other guy is the one talking, I assume that means Gage is giving him the lead. Yay.

"Are you related to a Dr. D. Buchanan?"

I look at Gage, asking him with my eyes, *What the hell?* Then I turn to the other cop. "Yeah. He's my father."

My father who's dead to me.

"Did you know Kara Becker was taking classes with your father?"

Shaking my head, I respond, "*Lots* of people take my father's classes." And the reason is because his classes are easy. Who doesn't love to get an easy A in their college English classes? It's one of the reasons they wouldn't give him tenure.

Well, until they did.

"So, he's popular?"

Where are they going with this? "Look." I lean forward. "People love my dad's classes because he's an easy A."

The two officers turn to look at each other, then back at me. "So...." The other cop sounds hesitant. "Everyone ends up with an A in his classes?"

"Well, not *everyone*. You have to turn things in. But the majority get As and Bs."

The men look at each other again, like they're trying to communicate without words.

Gage asks this time, "Is this something you've seen firsthand or just heard?"

"Well, obviously I don't do his grades for him." He wanted me to, but I refused. How lazy can one man be? "That's the rumor around campus." I blow out a big gust of air and lean back. "So, why are you asking about my father?"

"No reason." Gage shrugs. "We're just trying to get to know more about our vic."

"Vic?"

"Victim."

"Ah."

The two men stand simultaneously, like it was choreographed, but my eyes are on Gage. I do the same and follow them to my front door.

"Thank you, Miss Buchanan." Gage again.

"No problem."

Shutting the door behind them, I turn and lean my back against it. "What was that about?" Do they think my dad knows something about Kara's murder?

There's no way....

It's not possible. My father's way too self-absorbed to know or care about what's going on with his students.

Stepping into my living room, I can't decide what to do next. I know I need to shower, but Dad took all of my toiletries. The memories of last night rush back, and I'm overcome with anger again. I curl my hands into tight fists.

Taking in calming breaths, I relax my hands and decide on a plan of action. Picking up my purse, I shove my phone inside and grab my keys, I leave my apartment and jog down the steps to my car.

Well, to where I *thought* I left my car.

And then I realize. "That motherfucker." He took my car!

Reaching into my purse, I extract my phone to send my asshole of a dad a message. When I press the Home button, a message appears on the screen: *No longer in service.*

"Fuck!" My voice is so loud, I draw some attention from a few people in the parking lot, but I don't care. My eyes burn, which means there are tears making their way forward. I close my eyes in an attempt to focus because I refuse to cry. Not over this.

"It's okay," I say softly. "You've got this." And thanks to Ames having one of the best city bus services in the country, I'll just hop on CyRide to get where I'm going. "No problem."

Once I'm on the bus, my mind is numb. All I can think of is how desperate my father has become. Well, that's not all I can think about. No, I'm also pondering how I'm going to show him, once and for all, that I don't need him.

At my stop, I look down at the worthless phone I'm still clutching. I decide, in that moment, to leave it behind, in the seat. There's nothing personal on it; I was always careful about that. No, it's better to let someone who doesn't have the latest device use it.

In the store, I gather the things I need like shampoo, tooth-paste, and a toothbrush, which reminds me that I need a hair-brush. Along with that I find deodorant, some panties, a sweatshirt, a pair of jeans, leggings, a couple of tees, and a few tops. Once it's all rung up, the cashier gives me my total. Opening my wallet, I stare at the debit card my father gave me a few years ago, the one that goes with our joint account, and I just know. I know before I even try to use it that it's not going to work. Still, I run it through the card reader and wait.

"Oh," the cashier says, looking embarrassed—embarrassed for me. "It says declined."

"Mmhmm." Of course it does. Slipping that card back into my wallet, I take out my other one. The one I've been holding onto until it was time. "Let's try this one." I do my best to smile, but it's not real.

"Oh, good," she says with a relieved giggle. "That one worked."

Reaching out, I take the card and put it back in its spot.

With my bags in hand, I wait at the CyRide stop right outside the door. It doesn't take long, and luckily the bus is fairly empty right now. I move to the back of the bus and slide into a seat next to the window, leaning against it. The coolness of the glass feels good against my forehead.

This day has sucked.

The walk back to my apartment from the bus stop is slow thanks to the fact that I'm carrying six Target bags, a bag that holds a sub from a local sandwich shop, plus my purse. I trudge up the apartment steps, thinking about the shower I'm about to take. "Then I can eat," I mutter.

Setting everything down, I reach into my purse to find my keys. I remember throwing them back in when I discovered my car was gone. Locating my apartment key, I line it up with the lock and push, but it won't budge.

"No." I stare down at the key. Holding it up in front of my eyes, I make sure I've got the right one. Maybe I had it upside down. Placing the key in the lock, I try again.

"God. Fucking. Damn it." I say it loud enough for anyone on my floor to hear. Growling to myself, I hiss, "You just overplayed your hand, motherfucker."

"Daisy."

The voice catches me so off guard, I scream, jump back, and drop my keys. "What the hell? Gage?"

"Sorry." He moves closer, holding his hand out like he's trying to keep me from falling over. "I didn't mean to startle you."

"Well, you did." I look over at him and see Kara's door is open. "Were you in Kara's apartment?"

"Yeah." He nods. "I was waiting for you."

Another spy. God, I'm so sick of this crap. "Stalking me?" I spit.

He throws his head back like he's shocked at my words. "Absolutely not. I was worried about you."

Scoffing, I bend to retrieve my keys along with my bags. Turning, I start the walk back down the steps.

"Daisy."

I pause, turning my head to look at him. My lord, he's pretty in his blue jeans and blue Henley shirt. "What?" I'm not in the mood for this. "If you need to ask me more questions, it'll have to wait." Because now I need to find a new place to live faster than I'd anticipated.

"Where are you going?"

"Away."

"Away? Why?"

"He changed the locks." I nod at my door.

"Who did?"

"Daddy dearest."

"How?"

Why does he need to know? "Not now, Gage. *Not now.*" I move fast, stomping down the steps and out the door on my way back to the bus stop. There's a motel a few blocks away. I'll stay there for a night or two until I can figure out my next step.

I hear his footsteps before he says, "Daisy. Wait."

Stopping dead in my tracks, I rotate until I'm facing him. "What?"

"Where are you going?"

"To the bus stop."

He steps closer and bends slightly. I feel his hand touch mine, and then the bags in my right hand are gone. "Come on, sweetheart. I've got my car. I'll take you where you need to go." His voice is so soft, gentle.

And that's all it takes to put me over the edge. The tears start pouring out of my eyes, and I don't even try to stop them.

"Daisy?" I hear the bags rustling, but my eyes are closed. Then I feel him—or his arms, rather. They're wrapped around me in an embrace, and I honestly feel like it's the first time in forever anyone has hugged me. Shit. It only makes me bawl harder.

"Honey," he practically coos. I'm pressed against his hard chest, and all I want to do is snuggle against him for the rest of my life. "Shh, shh. It's gonna be okay."

I shake my head against him because I don't think I can talk right now. It doesn't feel like everything's going to be okay. Not ever.

"Sweetheart." He pulls away and I move with him, doing whatever I can to stay right where I am.

"Daisy." I open my eyes and see we're nose to nose. "Honey. It's gonna be okay."

Wiping at my eyes and nose, I sniffle and attempt to get my breathing under control. This time I nod.

"Let me take you. Where are you going?"

"Motel."

"You're going to a motel?"

I nod.

"Do you want to call your father?"

"No." I cough out the word thanks to the goop in my throat from all the crying. Okay, it's snot. Sorry. "I don't want to speak to him." Not now. Not tomorrow. Not *ever*.

With one hand, Gage holds mine. With the other, he picks up the shopping bags. "Let's go."

I have no fight left in me, so I go.

In his car, I buckle up and watch him do the same. "You hungry?" he asks.

"Not really." I still have a sub in one of my bags, though that doesn't even sound appealing anymore.

"How 'bout Blaze Pizza?"

I find a smile somewhere in all of my melancholy. "I could eat Blaze Pizza."

"Good, because I'm starving."

CHAPTER TWENTY-TWO

Gage

D riving to the restaurant, I spend half the time looking at the road and the other half checking on her. "You okay?"

"Yeah." She smiles at me, but it doesn't reach her eyes. "I will be."

At the pizza place, we line up to order. I watch and listen to Daisy order her pizza, and then it's my turn. The line goes quickly. I pay for both of us, hand her a cup for her drink, and locate a table near the back. Luckily we missed the dinner rush, so the restaurant is pretty dead. Once we've got our pizza, which is as good as she promised, I ask, "What happened?"

"My relationship with my father is... complicated."

I keep eating, not wanting to interrupt her.

"I got home last night to find my father had come in and taken my stuff."

"What do you mean? What stuff?" I look at her and realize she's still wearing the clothes from last night.

"Clothes, computer, toiletries, things like that." She scoffs. "He even took my sheets, blankets, pillows, and towels."

What the hell is that asshole doing? "Why?"

"He said it's because he's worried about me living across from a murder scene."

"He's right. It's not the safest place to live until we catch our killer."

"No." She shakes her head. "He doesn't care. My dad's playing a game with me."

"What kind of game?"

"He's trying to control me. To get me to move back in with him so he can control who I see." She looks at me pointedly. "I found a camera hidden in a bobblehead in my apartment."

What the hell? He's surveilling her? "You think he was watching you?"

"I do. Everything's in his name: the apartment, my car, my cell phone—heck, my bank account. Because I refused to move home, he cut off the phone and my debit card, and my car's gone."

That doesn't sound like something a concerned father would do. He's basically cut off her ability to run away or even reach out for help.

"So, what are you going to do?"

She shrugs. "I've got some other things in the works. I'm not broke or anything. I was smart and put money away in another account."

"Is it enough to—"

"It's enough," she says angrily.

Since we each ordered individual pizzas, I finish mine first, most likely due to the fact that she's been doing most of the talking, plus she's only picking at her pizza. "Well, until you figure things out, why don't you stay with me?" I offer, wiping my mouth with a napkin.

"No." she shakes her head. "That would be—"

"That would be perfect." I smile at her. "I've got a nice spare bedroom all set up."

She shakes her head again.

"You'd be doing me a solid, really."

"Oh yeah?" Her eyes are red, and her pretty nose is a little puffy, but she still nails the smirk. "How so?"

"Well, I'll be working late a lot, and you'd be, in essence, house sitting. You could keep Pepper company." Unless she's still afraid of my cat.

"Won't you get into trouble?"

I shrug. "I'll explain the situation to my boss. It'll be fine."

Hopefully.

I hold my breath, waiting for her answer. Then she says, "Okay. I can stay for a day or two."

"Great." I clap my hands together, then rub them. "So, you gonna eat that pizza?"

Pushing her plate into the middle, she smiles. "I just don't have any appetite right now."

I reach for a slice. "Good thing you didn't get anything weird on here like green olives." I shiver. Green olives on pizza is disgusting.

"Never." She giggles, and the sound gives me hope that she'll be okay.

CHAPTER TWENTY-THREE

Daisy

G age showed me to the guest room, which happens to be right next to his bedroom. It's a bit sparse with blue walls and a blue comforter on a full-sized bed. Even though there's no other decoration, it's still way better than sleeping at a Super 8 motel. Plus, the color blue is calming and cool. He placed my bags on the bed and left me alone, saying, "Feel free to shower. Bath is across the hall. Towels are under the sink."

So that's where I am. The warm water feels amazing as it runs over my head and down my body. I feel sore and like I'm hungover, but I haven't had a drop to drink. No, this is an emotional hangover, one that's left me exhausted.

Gage's bathroom is very nice. I saw it last night when I was here, and I was surprised at its spa-like feel. The shower is large, probably big enough for two. Which gives me thoughts of showers with Gage. Thoughts I need to forget about because he's not going to want anything to do with someone with as much baggage as I have. "Stop dreaming," I grouse.

Instead of feeling sorry for myself, I continue to peruse his design choices. The tile in the shower is a mix of gray and white mosaic. There are even some metallic pieces throughout that make it rather glamorous. The clear glass doors help make the bath feel larger. But the best part? The two showerheads. They're heavenly. Keeping in mind this isn't my house or my water bill, I reluctantly make my shower quick even though I'd love nothing more than to stand under the warm spray for an hour.

When I step out, my feet sink into a plush rug in a dark gray. They match his towels. Wrapping myself up, I step up to the vanity, the top of which is the same stone as in the kitchen. I'd guess granite. It's sleek and modern looking, and it matches the shower tile perfectly.

Reaching into one of my bags, I retrieve the toothbrush and toothpaste I purchased earlier today. I scrub my teeth, then run a brush through my hair. Tearing open the new package of underwear, I slip on the pink ones. I love pink. It's cheerful, and that's something I need right now. Since I forgot to buy pj's, I opt for leggings and one of the tees I bought. It'll have to do for now.

Before exiting the bathroom, I tidy up as best I can, leaving my toiletries out so I can use them tomorrow. "I hope you don't mind, Gage," I whisper to myself.

Opening the door, I take one step out and hit something solid. Gage's chest. "Oh." I laugh. "Sorry. I guess I wasn't watching where I was going." And now that I'm here, I'm in no hurry to move away from him.

"You feeling better, sweetheart?" He raises his hand like he wants to touch my face, but he drops it quickly.

Blinking, I look up into his eyes and smile. "Now that I've had a shower, yes. Definitely."

Neither one of us is moving. I could ask him to step aside, but as I said, I'm in no hurry. "Are you sure this is okay?" I hope he knows I'm referring to staying here.

"I'll talk to my captain tomorrow. I'm sure he'll understand."

He'll understand? That doesn't really sound like a ringing endorsement. "Are you sure?"

"Yeah." He smiles down at me. "I'm sure."

What are we doing? We're just inches apart in his narrow hallway, staring at each other. I feel like one of us should either make a move or ask the other one to back away. I'm for option A, by the way, but I'm not the kind of woman who makes first moves. Or second ones. But I've also never met someone like Gage Golden, nor have I ever stood as close to someone who looks and smells as good as him either. No, this is new. My life is a freaking disaster, so I'm hesitant to embarrass myself. On the other hand, my life's already a freaking disaster, so why not take the risk?

With courage I didn't know I had, I raise my hand and place it on the back of his neck. His blond hair tickles my fingertips, making this feel very real. I push myself up onto my tiptoes, my nipples pebbling as they brush over his chest. Sure, I've got on a tee, but there's no bra under it. He must feel it too because I hear his breath catch the second we make contact.

"You sure about this?" Gage asks in a husky voice. A voice that makes my nipples harder and my panties wet. "Because there's no going back."

"I'm sure."

And with that, his mouth is on mine. The kiss is best described as feverish. Passionate. I open for him the minute his tongue touches my lips. Mine moves past his until they're tangling and twirling around each other.

Okay, full disclosure. I'm not a virgin. Well, I'm not a virgin in the traditional sense. My hymen is gone, yes, but not thanks to a man. No, I took care of that with one of my toys a few years ago. But I'm more than ready to experience sex, especially if that sex is with Gage.

I wrap my arms around his neck so I can get even closer. That's when his palms find my ass. His touch is so good that I moan into his mouth. When I'm lifted off the ground, I hang on tight and then wrap my legs around his waist. I feel him then, right where I want him. Gage is hard and pressing against my center.

He pulls his mouth away from mine. I don't like the loss, so I chase it. "Taking you to my bedroom."

"Yes," I hiss, then latch onto his lips again. How have I lived so long without this man's mouth?

He's carrying me down the short hallway into his bedroom. I haven't been in there yet, so I have no idea what it looks like. It could be a war zone for all I care.

We fall onto the bed together, and his hand moves from my bottom to beneath my shirt. When his palm touches my stomach, I squeak. His hand is warm as it slides up to my breast.

"Touch me," I hiss again. "Please." God, I sound like a hussy, but like I said before, I. Don't. Care.

"You sure?" Gage kisses my cheek, then down to my neck. He sweeps his tongue right below my left ear, which feels so good that I whimper.

"Positive." Reaching down, I feel for his hand beneath my shirt and pull it up until it's cupping my right boob. "Please."

The growl that comes out of Gage's mouth is hot and goddamn sexy. When he pushes up to his knees and reaches for the bottom of my shirt, I push up as well to help him get rid of my stupid clothing. As soon as I'm topless, I reach for his shirt, but his mouth is on my nipple so fast, there's no time. And now I don't care if he has clothes on or not.

Flopping back down onto the bed, I arch into him. I want him to take my entire breast into his mouth, but since my boobs are bigger than average, that's not possible. I run my fingers through his hair as I watch him. Holy hell, he's really into this. His eyes are squeezed shut like he's concentrating hard on my nipple.

He moves over to the other breast, and I watch him work equally as hard on that one.

"Gage." I don't know why I speak his name. I think it's because I want to remember this. I want to remember the night I was with Gage Golden, and saying his name makes it real.

Reaching down, I find the edge of his tee and begin to pull. *Now* I want him naked. I'm ready for this.

Taking the hint, Gage takes one last swipe at my left nipple and pushes up again. He reaches back behind his head and pulls at his shirt. As it rises, it reveals a solid stomach that looks hard and soft at the same time. My hand is on him without thinking. I was right. His stomach is hard, but his skin's soft. The strip of blond hair that runs from his navel down into his sweatpants is my focus. Touching the hairs, one finger follows the trail down to the edge of his pants. I grasp the string and tug.

His erection is pressing against the fabric and only just below the band of his pants. As I prepare to reach inside, Gage takes hold of my hand, which confuses me. When I look up at him, he smiles.

Thank goodness.

His breathing is labored, as is mine. "Give me a minute," he says, touching my face.

I nod because I'm not sure what to say.

His eyes move from my face to my neck and finally rest on my chest. "You've got beautiful breasts, Daisy."

See? Did you hear him? He said breasts instead of tits. Not that I mind the other word, it's just Gage Golden is... well, I'd say he's a gentleman, but hopefully he's a dirty one.

"Thank you," I say, but what I'm actually thinking is *Now pull them and pinch them.*

He must read my mind because the next thing I know, two of his fingers are touching one of them. When he pinches, then pulls, I begin to wriggle.

"You like that, honey?"

"Yeah." I sound all breathy now. "Do it again."

With both hands, one on each, he does it again. And again. It's making me crazy.

"Gage," I whine. "Please."

"What do you want, Daisy? Tell me."

"Everything. Do everything to me."

"Fuck." With that, Gage has my leggings and underwear off in two seconds flat. I open my legs like the hussy I mentioned earlier. "Such a pretty pussy, Daisy."

And there it is. My dirty gentleman.

"Yeah."

Okay, I don't know what "Yeah" means right now since I've never really given my lady parts a good look before, but I like this Gage. I like him a lot.

"So fucking wet." His finger slides through my center slowly like he's savoring it. "Do I make you wet, honey?"

"Yes." *Now stop toying with me and fuck me or something.*

But I don't say it. I want him to take the lead—this time, at least. Instead, I scoot a little closer, encouraging him. When I feel something begin to slide inside of me, I push up onto my elbows so I can watch him. One of his fingers is pressing in, then out. When his thumb circles my clit, my hips move to his rhythm and my body begins to thrum. A tingle starts at my center and radiates out.

"Faster," I pant.

Gage's hand moves faster as his mouth latches onto my breast again. God. I'm so close. Lying back, I grasp his hair and pull on it hoping he understands my urgency. "So close."

I feel a change. His finger feels larger. Two fingers? It's then that the orgasm hits me.

"Yes!" I cry loudly. "Yes," I repeat but softer. I look up to see Gage gazing down at me. I lift my head and kiss him softly.

"How did that feel?" he asks sweetly.

How does he think it felt? The question makes me laugh. "Terrible."

"Oh. Wow. Sorry." He smirks.

Now it's his turn. Sliding my hand down, I reach into his sweatpants and moan again. The guy is bigger than any of my vibrators. Way bigger.

Gage's breath catches at my touch. When I stroke up and down his shaft, he chokes out, "You sure?"

"I'm sure."

When he stands, I push up again so I can watch. With his thumbs in his waistband, he slowly slides the pants down until his erection pops free.

"Whoa."

Gage sends me a beaming smile. "Hang on." Just then, he turns and walks over to a dresser near the door. The sight of his perfectly round ass makes me drool. When he returns, he has a condom in his hand. Placing the gold package in his mouth, he tears it open. I watch as he places it over the head and rolls it down.

This is it. I'm about to do *it* with Gage Golden.

With one knee on the bed, he grasps my ankle and holds my legs open so he can slide between my legs. I help him with my other leg, wrapping it around his waist.

"You sure, Daisy?"

"More than sure." I want him inside me. Now.

Looking down, Gage places himself at my entrance and slowly presses in.

He's big. Definitely very big. I hold my breath, expecting to feel pain, but that's not what happens. By the time he's seated all the way, I release the breath and smile. He feels good. Really, *really* good.

"Okay?" he asks, his voice sounding strained.

"Yeah."

And then it begins. He starts off slow, in, out. When I lift my hips to meet him halfway, it must be the right thing to do because his slow in-and-out changes into hard thrusts. Wonderfully passionate thrusts.

"There," I purr the second he hits the right spot.

"There?" he says with a pant.

"Yeah."

With the skill of a man who's had lots of sex, which I try not to think about, he begins to pound into me harder and in the right spot until I'm flying off into the universe. Stars are swirling around my head just as Gage moans his own release.

With both of us out of breath, he lowers himself until he's lying next to me. Wrapping his arms around me, he pulls me into him until we're face-to-face. "That was amazing," Gage says, kissing my eyelid.

"It was."

His palm is on my back, rubbing it up and down several times. When he stops, his palm is resting on my left ass cheek. I love how it feels.

That's when I hear him. His breath has evened out, and he's snoring a little. It's cute.

Reaching down past our feet, I grasp the comforter that I now see is the same blue color as the one in the spare bedroom and pull it over us. I spend a few minutes gazing at the beautiful man next to me. I refuse to think of tomorrow, though. Something tells me tomorrow is going to change everything.

CHAPTER TWENTY-FOUR

Gage

It's my fault. I let it happen. I should have stopped it in the hallway, but damn, her mouth, that body pressed against mine... how could I refuse her? She said, "Please," for shit's sake. When a woman asks you to fuck her and she says, "Please," you fuck her.

"Shit." I run my fingers through my hair. What was I to do? I wanted her as bad as she wanted me. Maybe more. I mean, my dick's hard whenever she's around, and while it's not necessarily good, it's just the way it is. God, her scent alone drives me crazy. I feel like a feral animal around her, like I can't control how my body responds to her. It wants her. *I* want her.

So now I'm standing outside my own front door, dreading what I have to do. And all of it because of my job.

You see, when I went to work this morning, I knew I had to clear everything with Captain Billings. I waited until the end of the day, needing the time to figure out what I was going to say. Things didn't go as I'd hoped. Not at all.

I sat in Captain Billings's office waiting for him to get off the phone, ready to tell him about Daisy and me. And while I'd told her last night that it was going to be okay, I wasn't so sure.

As soon as he hung up, he leaned over his desk, placed his elbows on top, and said, "That was Social Apartments' management. They're sending over the footage from the elevator."

"Finally," I grunted. "Did they give you any indication what was on the tape?"

"No." He shook his head. "We'll have to wait and see." He nodded. "So, what can I do for you?"

Clearing my throat, I started at the beginning. When I got to the part where I explained why she was staying at my place, I glanced at the captain and winced. His face said everything I needed to know.

"What the fuck, Golden?" He stood abruptly and pointed at my face. "That's against fucking protocol, and you goddamn know it."

I nodded. I did know it.

"She's a fucking eyewitness," he continued.

"We already know Tayler Soren—"

Shaking that off, Captain Billings shouted, "That's not official yet. The D.A. hasn't dropped the charges against her."

But they will. "I know. It's just—"

"You're thinking with your dick, Golden. That's unacceptable." He stepped around his desk until he stood next to me as he glared down at me. "Get her the fuck out of your house. Today. Or you're off this case."

So that's why I'm standing at my own front door, dreading this conversation I've got to have with Daisy. Before I overthink it, I unlock my door and step inside to the smell of something delicious cooking. When I look up, I see her in my kitchen working away at something.

Fuck. She cooked for me.

"Hey," she says with her pretty smile. "I hope you're hungry."

I am. I'm starving. *For her.*

Clearing my throat, I return her smile as I step closer to the kitchen. "It smells delicious."

"I made meatloaf. My mom's recipe."

Goddamn. I love meatloaf.

I scan the kitchen. It's a mess with pans, bowls, and utensils everywhere. The sight makes my heart jump in my chest. My kitchen has never looked so good. And seeing Daisy... fuck, she's beautiful with her dark hair piled on top of her head and her over-sized glasses resting on the tip of her pretty nose.

She's doing this for me.

Well, fuck Captain Billings. I'm not giving her up. Someone else can catch a killer. This right here is what I've been searching for my entire life. And no, I'm not searching for a woman who'll cook for me. I'm searching for everything this represents. With Daisy here, this isn't just a house. It's a home.

"I also made homemade mashed potatoes."

Jesus. She's going to kill me. "Real mashed potatoes?" I haven't had those in years.

"As real as they get." She beams. "I also made a loaf of bread, but it looks sort of sad." She holds up a loaf pan. The bread looks golden brown from here.

Stepping up behind her, I wrap my arms around her middle, lean down, and kiss her neck. Peeking over her shoulder, I get a closer look at the bread. She's right, it's a tad deflated and wrinkled. "I'm sure it still tastes good." Because, damn, it smells good.

She smells good.

Now that her body is against mine, I'm sure she can feel me because, of course, I'm hard.

"Gage." Her voice sounds soft and sexy.

"Yeah." I kiss her neck again before swiping my tongue over that spot.

I feel her hand touch one of mine that's wrapped around her waist. When she tugs on it, I let her move it up and up until I'm cupping her breast.

"You want me?" I ask, hoping her answer is "Yes." *Tell me you want me. For longer than today.*

"All I've done today is think about you." Her voice is husky now.

I move my right hand from her waist into her jeans. They're a little snug, but I'm still able to make it inside and down between her legs. "You're fucking soaked."

"Told you," she breathes. "All I've done today is think—"

My mouth is on hers before she can finish that sentence. I press a finger inside of her, which causes her to moan into my mouth.

This is too much. Too overwhelming. Pulling my hand out of her pants, I bring my other one down until I've worked the button loose on her jeans. Unzipping them, I've got her jeans and panties down to her knees before you could say "Meatloaf." I make quick work of my own pants and boxers until I'm free and hard against her ass.

"This okay, honey?" I murmur.

"Yes."

"Bend over. Hold on to the counter."

"O-Okay."

With my palms on her hips, I pull her closer to me. Lining myself up, I'm inside so fast, I feel dizzy. She felt like a fist on my cock last night, but this way, from behind, it's like a velvet vise.

"Fuck," I spit as I pull out and thrust back in hard. "Hold on tight." This is gonna be fast.

"It feels good, Gage."

With every thrust in, she presses back. It's like we're doing a well-choreographed dance—one we've done a million times before. But this is only the second time for us, and it's so. Fucking. Good.

I'm close. Reaching around her, I find her clit and circle it fast, then slow. When I give it a little pinch, she comes, and I feel it down to my toes. She's pulsing around me, which puts me there. With a growl, I come hard inside her.

Oh fuck.

Inside her.

"Daisy?" I look down at the place we're joined, watching as I seep out of her entrance. It's confusing me because the animal in me loves the idea of Daisy and me mating. But the human male in me, who's always responsible and thoughtful, is fucking disgusted with himself. "I didn't wear a condom." I pull out and reach into the drawer next to her right arm for a clean dishtowel. Pressing it against her, I wipe away the excess. Folding it onto itself, I hold it there, waiting.

She's silent for way too long before she finally says, "Oh."

"I'm sorry."

She reaches down and pulls up her pants. "I just finished my period. I'm sure it's okay."

"If not...." *If not, I'll be there for you.* Except I don't say it.

"No worries." She shrugs. Turning to face me, she smiles, but it doesn't reach her eyes. "I guess you like meatloaf." Then she giggles and I'm able to breathe again. "I'll have to remember that."

Bending down, I kiss her softly. "I'm not going anywhere." I hope she understands what I mean.

"Okay."

I'm going to take that as a good sign.

"Dinner will be ready in a few minutes if you need to, um...." She looks down at me. I'm still naked from the waist down.

"I'll go clean up and change." I reach down and pull up my pants and boxer briefs. "Back in five."

CHAPTER TWENTY-FIVE

Daisy

I'm not on birth control. Why would I be? I mean, before Gage Golden knocked on my door, I practically hid from the world. Hell, the night he discovered her... Kara, I barely opened my door.

Now all I want to do is be *out*. I want to be with people, to see the world, to experience all the things I've missed out on. I'm not sure a baby would fit into this revised worldview, but like I told him, my period ended less than a week ago. I'm sure I'm okay.

Even if I'm not, I could live this life. You know, the one where I do my thing all day while he's at work. Sometimes I could make him dinner, sometimes he would cook, but every day we'd do what we did in the kitchen just now. Because wow-wow-wow, that was sexy and hot and it felt so good. No way can my toys replicate that. Not in a million years. No, Gage and me, we're in sync when it comes to sex. *Very* in sync.

It's too bad it won't last. Nothing this good ever does. To be honest, I was surprised he came home and did what he did. I figured he'd go to the station, tell his boss what was going on here, and be forced to choose between me and his job. But I guess he was right. Everything was okay there.

Shaking off my negative thoughts, I smile as Gage eats a third portion of, well, everything. "You like it?" I want to laugh at my question because it's obvious he does. He's barely spoken since he took his first bite.

"Mmhmm," he says, nodding. Shoveling a scoop of potatoes in his mouth, he closes his eyes and nods again. "Good."

Oh, he said a word. I giggle to myself because it feels wonderful to do something for another person—one who appreciates the gesture.

I didn't set out today to be Betty Crocker for Gage. No, I left right after he did and hopped on the bus en route to a phone store to replace the one I left on CyRide. This time, the phone's in *my* name, and I'm the only one who has access to it. I made sure to choose a different service provider, just in case.

After that, I walked to my favorite thrift store to shop for more clothing. The things I bought yesterday are fine, but I needed more since the weather is turning colder. I found several sweaters, a wool skirt, and a pair of retro-looking shoes, then moved on to another large chain store to buy more underwear and a black bra and some tights. As I passed the grocery section of the store, I decided I would cook Gage a good meal. It was the least I could do, you know other than sleep with him, since he was letting me stay at his place. But I didn't sleep with him for *him*. That was all for me.

Making meatloaf and mashed potatoes was a no-brainer—it was my mom's favorite meal, and because she loved it, so did I. My attempt at homemade bread was all my idea, though. I didn't ever recall her making bread, but how hard could it be, right?

It turns out it's harder than it looks. Not even YouTube videos helped me.

Reaching out, I pick up my slice of bread with butter slathered on top and bite. "Mm," I say aloud. "That's not bad."

"Good," Gage grunts again, and I laugh.

"What?" he asks with his mouth full.

"Nothing." I smile. "I'm glad you like it."

I watch him swallow his bite. After drinking a sip of water, he smiles at me. "I do. It's the best meal I've ever eaten."

For some reason, his words make me blush.

"I'm happy to hear that."

I really am.

CHAPTER TWENTY-SIX

Gage

We've eaten dinner, done the dishes, and now we're sitting on the sofa watching a sitcom. It feels so damn domestic. I should probably cringe at the notion and run for the hills, but that's not the way I feel about it. No. I'm content. Happy, even. I mean, my stomach is full—*very* full—and my arm is wrapped around my girl, who's cuddled into me and laughing at something funny on TV. Pepper Anderson is curled up in Daisy's lap like she's meant to be there, all while Daisy strokes the top of her yellow head.

This is the life.

At least it's the life I've always wanted. A life I only imagined with one other person, but she's better off where she is. I know that now, because I was never supposed to be with Quinn Maxwell. No, I'm sure I was always meant to meet Daisy.

"Well, that was a funny show."

"It was," I say absently as I run my fingers over a strand of hair that must've fallen out of her bun. It feels silky as it slides along my hand. "I've never seen it. I'm usually on patrol at this time of night."

Daisy turns her body until we're facing each other. "That's right. I forgot about that. You were on patrol that night."

"I was."

"So, after this investigation, you'll go back to working nights?" Her dark brows furrow, and her nose scrunches up. It's fucking adorable.

"I assume so. Why? Does that bother you?"

I'm waiting for a response, but all she's doing is blinking. I can see worry in her eyes. "No. Of course not. Are we...?" she stammers. "Is this...?"

Taking her hands in mine. "I think we are, and I think this is, but only time will tell."

She's searching my eyes, though for what, I'm not sure. "It's moving fast."

"Is that a bad thing?" I don't think so.

Turning back to her spot cuddled up against me, she says, "I don't know." Picking up the remote, she presses the Guide button. "It's only eight. Let's watch something else."

I guess we're done talking about that, which is okay with me because it got heavy real fast, and I don't have any answers for us right now. Neither of us does.

As she slides through channels, I spot something I've wanted to check out. "Let's watch *The Great Gatsby*."

"Ha-ha," she deadpans. "Funny."

"What? Why not. It's got that Leo guy in it, right? I heard it's good."

Daisy presses her face into my arm and groans. Or maybe growls is a better word.

"What?"

Pushing away from me, she looks me square in the eye and says, "I'm named after the heroine in *The Great Gatsby*, although 'heroine' denotes someone good or heroic, and she was definitely neither of those things."

"Okay," I say, though I'm not sure where she's going with this. "So, no to the movie?"

I guess what I said was funny because she laughs. "Fine. I haven't seen this version of the story, so if you want to watch it...." She looks me square in the eye, "But if you think I'm anything like that character—"

Raising both hands, I pronounce, "I promise. No comparisons."

"Because my father is an asshole, and it started the day I was born. He cursed me with this name, and he did it on purpose."

"Why? What do you mean?"

"Because his father, Rochester Buchanan, who was named after the character Edward Rochester from *Jane Eyre*, named my father after a character in an Oscar Wilde novel. His *only* novel."

"Why is that a curse?"

"Because." She sighs. "He's named after the main character in *The Picture of Dorian Gray*."

"What's wrong with that?" She's going to have to spell this out for me.

"Wow. Okay. So, *The Picture of Dorian Gray* is about this young, wealthy man who has a painting of himself commissioned. The artist is so taken with Dorian's good looks, he becomes obsessed with him. It ends up being this artist's masterpiece. In the course of the sittings, Dorian's introduced to another man, a lord. I can't remember his name, but this lord shows Dorian the dark side of London."

"Dark side?"

"You know, drugs, prostitutes, things of that nature. The London underbelly."

"Ah, I see."

"Anyway, Dorian gets so deep into this underbelly, it goes on for a long time, and he ends up murdering someone. But the part about this story that made it so strange was that no matter how old or debauched Dorian got, it never showed. Years pass and he never ages or changes. None of his excess affects him. Instead, all of his bad, terrible deeds appear in the painting."

"Huh? How?"

She shrugs. "Something about the painting. It takes on all of Dorian Gray's ugliness."

"What happens?"

"Well, Dorian hides the painting, but he still visits it. In the end, he stabs the painting, and it kills him."

"What? It kills him? How?"

"Well, by stabbing the painting, he's stabbing himself." She nods. "Blood even seeps from the painting."

I raise a brow. "Wow. That sounds like a great story. That'd make a great movie."

"They've made it into a movie. It's old, though."

"Fascinating. Maybe we could find it somewhere and watch it."

"As long as we don't have to watch *The Great Gatsby*, I'm all in."

"Maybe I'll just read the book." I give her a smirk.

Daisy's head hits the back of the sofa. "No. Please don't. Trust me, Daisy Buchanan is the worst person in the world."

"Worse than Dorian Gray?"

She purses her lips. "Well, no. But she's pretty bad."

"Fine. Let's see where that Dorian Gray movie is. If I have to get one of those online movie subscriptions, I will."

"Let's check. Do you have a computer?"

"Yep. Let me get it."

CHAPTER TWENTY-SEVEN

Daisy

In the end, we found a movie called *Dorian Gray* that was filmed in 2010.

"Told you it was disturbing," I say as the credits roll.

"It was, but what a creative story."

I'll give Oscar Wilde that. "Wilde was ahead of his time, really."

"Why would your grandfather name his child after a character like that?"

I shrug. "I never met him, but I'm going to guess he did it for the same reason my dad named me after an F. Scott Fitzgerald character—he loved Oscar Wilde."

"Hmm." Gage looks off like he's thinking. "If I had a child, I think I'd name it something average. You know, like John."

I giggle, but I have to ask, "You want kids?"

Smiling down at me, he nods. "I do. You?"

"I wouldn't mind. I'd want more than one, though. Being an only child sucks."

He laughs. "Yeah, well, I've got a brother, and he's a pain in the ass, so there's that."

"Why? What's he do?" This is the first real personal information I've gotten from Gage. It's nice.

"He's always getting into trouble."

My eyes grow round. "Like legal trouble or lady trouble?"

Chuckling, he takes my hand and holds it. "Both."

"Wow. And you're even a cop. Does he live around here?"

"Nah. I'm from Missouri originally. He still lives there, in the town where we grew up."

"What about your parents?"

"My dad died a few years ago. My mom's still in the same town. They live next door to each other, actually."

"That's nice for her. He can do things for her."

Scoffing, Gage explains, "It's the other way around. I'm pretty sure she still does his laundry."

"No!" I slap Gage's firm chest. "How old *is* he?"

"Twenty-four." He pauses. "No, twenty-five now."

"Close to my age. Old enough to do his own laundry." I mean, seriously.

Chuckling, he leans down and kisses me quickly. "You're right." Moving a rogue piece of hair out of my face, he adds, "I think she likes to do it. It makes her feel needed or something."

"She sounds nice." I close in on him and give him a kiss. "I'm sorry about your dad."

"Thanks." Gage kisses me again, this time a little deeper. "He was a good man."

"Like you?" We kiss again, a little longer this time.

"Better." I feel Gage's fingers slide around my neck and into my hair. His tongue sweeps against my lip, so I open for him. It's getting heated fast. Moving closer, I crawl over him until I'm straddling his lap.

"You're addictive, Mr. Golden."

Kissing down my neck, he whispers. "So are you, Miss Buchanan." Sliding his hand beneath my shirt, he skims over my lacy bra. "Let's go to bed."

"Yeah." I nod. "Let's."

CHAPTER TWENTY-EIGHT

Gage

"There." I point to the monitor on Dan's desk. We're watching the footage from the elevator in Kara Becker's building. "He's the only one who entered via the elevator during the estimated time of death."

"Yeah, but who is he? It's impossible to tell thanks to the black trench coat and big hat. We can't see shit," grumbles Dan. "Was it raining that day?"

I shake my head. "It was chilly but no rain." I watch the footage again.

Finch points. "Who wears that kind of coat these days? And that hat. It looks like something from an old black-and-white movie. What do they call those?"

"A fedora," Dan replies .

"A fedora?" Finch sounds perplexed. "Seriously. Who wears a hat like that?" Snapping his fingers, he holds one up. "An old guy. That's who."

Looking down at the screen, I see it's stopped. "Play it again."

Dan starts the video again, and all three of us lean closer. "He's got on dress shoes too."

"It's grainy, but you can tell they're shiny."

Finch mumbles something about old guys and shiny shoes, but I ignore it. The truth is, he's right. Those are two things an older man would wear.

"Shit." I push up to full height. "You can't see his face. Hell, you can't even tell what color his hair is."

"I'd guess he's at least six feet tall."

Dan glares at Finch. "How are you getting that? We're looking at this guy from above." Because the camera is mounted in the top corner of the elevator, our point of view is a little skewed.

Finch shrugs and points to the top of our guy's head. "I could go measure the elevator and see if I'm right."

"Yeah." I nod. "Anything would help." Dan states absently as he fiddles with the controls trying to make the picture clearer.

We watch it one more time, but nothing jumps out to identify the mystery man.

"So that was a whole lot of nothing," I mutter angrily. "I had hopes for that." I point at the screen. The one good thing it does is give Tayler Sorenson a better defense. If it came to it, she could show there were other possible suspects, which means there's reasonable doubt.

Turning to Finch, I ask, "Did you get in touch with Falco?"

"Yeah. Finally." He sighs. "He called me back last night."

"And?"

"He claims he hadn't seen our vic for several months. I asked him to come down today so we can print him and talk to him in person."

"Good." I nod. *Smart thinking, rookie.* I want to get a look at this guy too. "What time's he gonna be here?"

"He didn't say. I'll follow up with him, though."

"Good."

"What about the grades, Dan?"

The detective sighs. "ISU won't release any information about Dr. Buchanan's grades. They're confidential, and I think we'd have a hard time convincing a judge for a warrant because our reason for wanting them is flimsy as fuck."

He's right, and it's probably nothing, anyway. I mean, Dr. Dorian Gray Buchanan is very well respected.

"Hey... wait." I reach for the folder we took on our trip to Stuart yesterday. Opening it, I search for the notes from Kara's journal. "DG." Looking at Dan, I ask, "Did you ever figure out who DG was?"

"Nope."

"Dr. Buchanan's name is Dorian Gray Buchanan."

"Wasn't Dorian Gray a movie?" Finch asks.

"It was a book by Oscar Wilde." I nod. "And also a movie."

Dan shakes his head. "Wouldn't he be listed as DB if it was him?"

My shoulders slump. "Probably." Not giving up, I stand up to find the actual journal. When I can't find it, I look at Dan. "Where's the journal?"

"Captain's got it."

What? "Why?"

Dan shrugs.

I'm up and out of my chair in a second and in front of the captain's door in five more. Knocking, I listen for him to tell me to enter. When he finally speaks, I open the door and step inside. "I need the journal."

"Why?"

Wow, okay. "I've got a theory."

With a sigh, he opens his desk drawer and withdraws a pink leather-bound book. "Bring it back. Her father's concerned Kara's personal thoughts are going to get out there."

Ignoring him, I take hold of the journal and tug it from his hands.

What is it with the captain and Kara's father?

Back in the conference room, I slide back into my seat, open her journal to page one, and read.

~

OPENING THE DOOR TO MY HOUSE, I'M TEMPTED TO pronounce, "Honey, I'm home," but I don't. I sniff the air, hoping she's cooking again, but smell nothing new or delicious.

Not only that. It's quiet. Too quiet.

"Daisy?" I say loud enough that if she's in one of the bedrooms, she'd hear me. When I get no response, I walk past the kitchen and down the short hallway to the bedrooms and bath. Peeking into the spare room, I see it's empty. The bathroom door is open, so I know she's not in there. Pushing open the door to my bedroom, I hold my breath, hoping she's already in my bed. Preferably naked. Sadly, that's not the case. My bed is still made from this morning and empty.

"Daisy?" I say again just for the hell of it.

Then I remember the deck. She could be out there. Moving out of my bedroom, I walk through the kitchen to the back door. Opening it, I step onto my wooden deck that overlooks a decent-sized yard. "Daisy?"

Still nothing.

In the kitchen, I spot a note. I hold my breath again, worried it's going to tell me she's leaving—a goodbye note. Reaching out, I pick it up and slowly bring it close enough for me to read.

Gage,
   I'm running errands. I'll be ~~home~~ back later.
   Daisy

Relief washes over me except for one thing. The way she crossed off "home" and replaced it with "back" bothers me. A lot. *Why can't this be her home too?*

Which reminds me. Captain Billings asked me point-blank today if I'd dealt with the Daisy issue. I merely nodded.

"Good," he said, then walked away.

Yes, I lied to my commanding officer. But it can't be helped.

Changing into sweats and a tee, I grab a beer from the fridge and return to the deck. It's a nice night. There's a little chill in the air, but nothing that will bother me. Sitting in one of my lounge chairs, I sip and think about today—about the investigation.

Bryant Falco finally showed up. With his father. And a lawyer.

Strange. Why would he bother bringing a lawyer with him? Unless he's got something to hide. But in the end, the interview was worthless. He claims he hasn't seen Kara for months and that they weren't dating, just sleeping together. He claims she was clingy and, with a nonchalant shrug, added, "She's kind of a bitch."

She was. Kind of a bitch, I mean.

When we asked him where he was at the time of the murder, his father interjected, "He was home, with us, visiting."

It's not that I don't believe him, but I don't believe him. Finch is going to dig a little deeper into Bryant Falco. Hopefully he'll find out if he was, in fact, back home in Des Moines. Even if he was, it's only thirty-five minutes away. He could have driven to Ames and back before his father even knew he was gone.

Which gives me an idea.

Me: Did we see anyone matching Falco's description entering the building that night?

Dan: We weren't looking for him, but now that we've seen him. I'll look again.

Me: Thanks.

Dan: No problem. Now quit working and have a beer.

Me: Yes, sir.

Dan: Good. Life's too fucking short. You take this job too seriously, trust me, you'll wake up and what you considered your real life is gone.

Wow, that's the most the guy has ever said to me. And it was personal.

Me: Got it. Thanks. **says as he takes a drink of beer**
Dan: Ha. Good.

Placing my phone on the arm of the lounger, I lean back and sip my beer, wondering where the hell my girl is. I'd call her, but she doesn't have a phone.

"Shit." Now I'm going to worry.

CHAPTER TWENTY-NINE

Daisy

I get home around nine, much later than I'd anticipated, but it can't be helped. I had things to take care of today. Things that took time. "Hello?" I ask as I step into the house. "Gage?"

"In here."

By that I assume he means the bedroom since he's not in the living room or kitchen. With bags in hand, I stop in the spare bedroom and am about to set everything on the bed but notice the cat's asleep right in the middle. I'm not sure how I feel about that. Does he really need a cat? He's got me now.

Giving the yellow creature my best evil eye, I set the bags on the floor. When I turn, I catch a glimpse of myself in the little mirror above the dresser. I feel a gasp is in order because I look like I've been caught in a wind tunnel. My hair's a mess, my shirt's wrinkled, and my leggings... well, they're fine. I quickly search for my hairbrush to work out the knots and tangles. It hurts, but I get it done in no time.

Stepping up to his bedroom door, I knock.

"Why are you knocking?"

I jump, startled, because I didn't expect him to open the door.

Placing my hand over my heart to get it to calm down, I laugh. "Wow. You scared me."

"Sorry."

It's right then I notice Gage. Well, I notice what he's wearing: a pair of dark gray sweatpants. Nothing else. The heat of a blush creeps up from my neck onto my cheeks. I know I shouldn't be blushing because I've seen this man naked, but still....

"You blushing, honey?"

"No." The lie makes my cheeks even warmer. "Yes."

Leaning down, Gage kisses me softly. "You're pretty when you're all pink."

Oh shit. Here it comes again.

"Glad you're *home*." I hear emphasis in the last word. And I know why. When I wrote that note, it felt weird to call Gage's house home, so I crossed it off. I probably should have rewritten the note, but I was in a rush.

In an attempt to change the direction of this conversation, I smile up at him. "Me too."

"Where'd you go?"

"I had some business to take care of."

"Like?"

"I got a new phone for one. I'll be sure you have my new number later." I also did some more shopping, looked at a couple apartments, and bought a car. A used one, but it's reliable-ish and should last me long enough for me to get the rest of my stuff in place. But I don't want to tell him all of that, so I just give him the obvious one. The one that's parked out on the street in front of his house. "Also some shopping. I bought a used car."

"A used car?" He sounds surprised. "By yourself?"

I'm not sure why, but his comment bugs me. "Yeah. By myself."

"Where'd you get it?" He sounds a tad judgmental.

Déjà vu is hitting me. My dad questions me like this. "From a student." Who was desperate for cash. I feel like we helped each other.

Gage chuckles. "Daisy. Have you ever bought a car before?"

"No." Duh.

"And you just decided to buy one today. By yourself?"

"Yep." I could tell him I did my research, but why bother?

Turning, I step out of his bedroom into the spare room. I'm very close to packing up my stuff and leaving. I think I was right in my note earlier. This isn't my home—just like my apartment wasn't my home.

"Daisy?" He's close. Probably standing in the doorway. "I'm sorry. I just thought about what I said to you and how I said it. I didn't mean to sound like an asshole male."

"Well, you did." I reach for one of my bags from earlier, trying to decide if I should empty it or fill it with the rest of my stuff.

When his arms wrap around my waist, I flinch. "Gage. Not now."

"Honey." He kisses my neck. "I'm sorry."

Sure he is.

"I shouldn't have said anything."

No shit.

I feel his hands on my waist, urging me to face him. I go ahead and do it. When he sits on my bed, he pulls me closer. "I mean it. I know I sounded like a macho jackass just now. I didn't mean to suggest that you didn't know what you were doing."

"Uh-huh." I still haven't looked him in the eye.

"Please look at me, honey."

I can't.

"Please?" he repeats.

Damn it. I turn my head just enough to look at him with my left eye. "Happy?"

"No. I won't be happy until you accept my apology, and even then, I'll feel like shit all night."

"You should." I'm just going to say what I need to say. "I don't need a guy telling me what to do, Gage. My dad's done that forever. Hell, he still thinks he can do it. It's *my* money, *my* car, and *my* decision." My voice is getting stronger the more I say. "So, even if the car I bought is a piece of junk, it's *my* piece of junk. I'll live with it like I've lived with all my decisions. You got me?" I'm pretty much yelling now.

"I do." Gage nods several times. "I get you. I'm sorry."

Breathing hard, I give him one nod. "Okay."

"Okay," Gage mimics me. "We good?"

"Yeah. We're good."

There are a few moments of the two of us just looking at each other. He's the one to break the silence. "Did you eat?"

God, this guy... he's *so nice.*

Shaking my head, I run my hand over my stomach. "Is there any meatloaf left?"

Gage looks sheepish. "No. I ate it for dinner." He pulls me closer, wrapping me up in his arms. "I'm sorry. I should have left you some."

"No. It's fine." I pat his chest. "I'll make a turkey sandwich or something."

"Let me make you something." His voice is extra soft, like he's making sure not to set me off again. Probably a good plan.

"You cook?"

"Some. I make a mean grilled cheese."

"You do?" I do my best to look impressed. "Well, then I'd love a grilled cheese sandwich."

"Come on." Gage takes my hand in his and pulls me into the kitchen. "Watch and learn, princess."

Princess? While I like the moniker, I'm definitely *not* a princess.

I watch Gage work in the kitchen, and it's pretty damn cute. Sure, I'm still a little miffed with him about the whole car thing, but I believe he's sorry. Like really sorry.

The sandwich is golden brown and oozing with cheese. He was right, he makes a mean one.

"Mm, good," I say after my first bite.

"Told ya."

I don't bother responding because I'm starving. Once I'm finished, I stand, taking the plate to the dishwasher. "Thanks, Gage."

"Welcome." He's standing too far away for me to touch, so I step closer, holding my hand out. I hope he takes it. When he does, I tug on his a little bit. "Come on. I'll give you a ride in my new kickass car."

"Yeah?"

"Yeah. But swear to God, Gage, if you say one negative thing, I'm leaving you to walk home."

He chuckles. "I won't say a word."

CHAPTER THIRTY

Gage

Her car's a piece of shit. There's no other way to describe it. Sure, it started up okay today, but I give it less than six months. Hell, I'd be surprised if it lasted three. I'd love to know how much she spent on it, but I'm afraid to ask. Lucky for her, my dad taught me and my brother about cars when we were younger. There's a good chance, though, that I won't be able to fix what ails that car. I can change her oil, rotate her tires, stuff like that, but that grinding noise you hear on every turn? That's going to need a professional.

And the dark smoke that puffs out of the exhaust pipe? Another job for a pro. But I do what she asked, keeping my mouth shut about what's wrong and only focusing on the good. "It's got power windows."

"Right?" She beams and nods at my door. "That one is a little wonky, but it still works."

I press the button for the window and watch as it is, in fact, wonky. It doesn't go all the way down, and when it stops, it's at an angle. But she's right. It works. "Nice," I say with a smile. One I'm forcing into place.

"The trunk's roomy too."

"Ah." I nod. "Good." I blink, trying to think of something to say. Finally I ask, "What do you plan to carry around in your trunk?"

She shrugs. "I don't know. It's just nice to have the room for whatever."

"It is."

And the fact that I've got a full-sized SUV in the driveway isn't a factor, I guess.

But maybe she's already planning on leaving. She could fit a lot of her belongings in the trunk, if that's the case.

"Daisy?" I ask as she pulls up to the curb in front of my house.

"Yeah?"

"Are you planning on staying with me?"

"Huh?" She jerks her head to her right to look at me. "What? For now? Or—" She swallows. "—forever?"

"I... I don't know." I'm not ready for her to leave.

"I looked at an apartment today."

"You did?" Where was that, I wonder.

"Yeah. I figured that'd be for the best."

"I see." I don't see, but I'm not sure what else to say.

"You didn't want me to live with you, did you?"

I don't reply. What can I say to that?

"Gage?"

"Honestly?" I look over at her. "I don't know *what* we're doing."

She reaches for the door handle and pulls. Nothing happens, so she uses her shoulder to force the door open. Before stepping out, she mumbles, "Oh. Right."

Those are the last two words either of us says until we're back inside my place. Our silence continues until it's time for bed. Are we going to sleep together? Should I ask her where she's sleeping? I listen as she does her nightly routine in the bathroom while I sit on my bed with my door half open. I didn't want to shut it and make her think I didn't want her to enter, but I didn't want to leave it wide open in case... in case she walks past it. Talk about awkward.

When the bathroom door clicks open, I hold my breath. And wait. Her feet pad across the hallway into the spare bedroom, and my heart sinks.

Wow, it hurts.

Choosing to hide my reaction, I slide down beneath my covers and switch off my bedside light. Closing my eyes tight, I try to think about something else rather than the sick feeling in my stomach.

"Gage?" Daisy's voice is soft. And close.

Clearing my throat, I say, "Yeah?" I turn my body to see her standing next to the bed.

"Do—" She stops. "Do you—"

"Yes." I reach out and take her hand. "Yes. I want you in my bed."

Her relief is obvious in the breath she just released. "Okay."

Scooting over, I pull the blanket and sheet back to make room for her. As soon as she's next to me, I drop the blankets over us, wrap my arm around her, and pull her close. Kissing her softly, I whisper, "I think I'll always want you in my bed, Daisy."

"Yeah?" I hear her sniffle.

"You crying, honey?"

"Maybe."

"Why?"

"Because... I didn't mean to hurt you earlier. I just don't know what I'm doing with my life. It doesn't mean I don't want you in it. It just means I'm not sure I'm ready to live with you."

"You're living with me now."

"No, I'm *staying* with you. That's different."

Semantics. "I guess."

Daisy snuggles up next to me, close enough for me to smell her hair. She used my shampoo. I like it.

"Thank you for not criticizing my car."

"No problem."

"And for not asking me how much I paid for it."

"Uh-huh." I still want to know.

"It was three hundred bucks."

"Oh." I release a gust of air out of relief. "Thank fuck."

She slaps my chest and giggles. "Jerk."

Before I say a word, I rehearse it in my head. "Next time, if you'd like me to, I'll car shop with you."

"If I'd like?"

"Only if you'd like. I know a little about cars."

"So do I." She giggles. "No I don't. But if it lasts me six months, I'll be ahead."

"I know a good mechanic...."

"No, Gage."

"Fine." And it is fine. But I hope she knows she can count on me if she stalls on the side of the road.

Her lips touch mine, and I sink into it. Her lips are so soft. They fit mine perfectly.

Everything about Daisy fits perfectly against me.

CHAPTER THIRTY-ONE

Daisy

Today's the day. I'm going to drive over to my dad's house while he's in class to see if I can get my stuff back. Before I go, I drive to campus to make sure he's there today. I spot his fancy Mercedes coupe in his usual spot and know he won't be home. Before I can change my mind, I speed over to his house on Timberland Road. It sits back from the road, secluded on a wooded lot. This wasn't the house I grew up in. No, that one was much more modest and closer to campus.

He bought *this* house after he got tenure and a lot of attention for his—*my*—writing. Hell, Mom didn't even get to live here.

I have a room here, though. He set it up with all of my old furniture from the little house. He painted the walls pink and bought a fluffy white comforter for the top of the bed. It's weird that he went to all that trouble and I've never slept a night in the place.

No matter.

I pull in front of one of the four garages. Attempting to put it into Park proves difficult since my gearshift isn't cooperating, so I put the thing into Neutral and press on the emergency brake.

At the front door, I ring the bell. I might as well cover my bases. When no one answers, I try the handle, but it doesn't budge. Taking out the key he gave me years ago, I press it into the lock and hold my breath, hoping it still works.

It does.

Pushing the door open, I sigh in relief that I made it inside. But that's short lived because the loudest fucking siren slash alarm sounds. It's so loud I have to cover my ears. I search left, then right for a control panel for the security system, but there isn't one. My ears still covered, I run into the adjacent dining room, looking for anything that will help me shut the damn thing off.

My God. It's so loud!

Turning left, I race down a short hallway into my father's office. A room he calls his "study." Eye roll. How pretentious, right?

Pushing open the french doors with one hand, I quickly cover my ears again. I scan the room and spot a keypad on his desk. Racing over, I stare down at a control box with the name Dynamic Security printed prominently at the top. Blinking at the alphanumeric keypad, I mutter, "What's the combination, Dad?"

Here's hoping it's a four-digit code. I choose to press in his birthday: 0871.

Nothing. The alarm is still screaming. Next I try: 081971 but it won't let me add two additional numbers. A four-digit code it is.

Next, I try Mom's middle name: Ruth

Damn. It didn't work.

I try my birthday: 0796

"Fuck!" I scream. But nobody can hear me. It's too loud.

Shit. What code would he use? He's an egomaniac, so it has to be something related to himself. It *has* to be.

I stare at the controller. "Think, Daisy. Think."

My God, the noise is so loud and piercing it's painful. Maybe I should just leave. Or I could put on some headphones or something. Anything to block out the sound.

I rotate on the spot looking at his office shelves, filing cabinets, the top of his desk, and the other furniture. Nothing here to cover my ears, unless.... Pulling open the top drawer in his desk, I push the contents around but don't spy earplugs or headphones. Next, I move to the drawers that run down the right side of his mahogany behemoth of a desk. Searching the top two results in nothing usable. However, just as I'm about to search the third drawer down, two things happen. One, I hear sirens sounding from somewhere outside his office window, and two, I spy something unexpected in the drawer.

Reaching in, I push aside a few papers and then hear "Freeze." I look up and see a cop standing in the open doorway, gun drawn and pointed at me, and looking quite angry. My first thought is how loud he must've just yelled, "Freeze," for me to hear him over this godforsaken alarm.

Why does my dad need an alarm system, anyway?

In the end, I do what I'm told. I freeze.

"Put your hands up," he shouts.

Once again I do as he says.

Before I can utter a word, my arms are wrenched behind my back and something is wrapped around my wrists. I hear a zipping sound and know I'm being cuffed with zip ties. They're so tight, I feel them digging into the skin around my wrists.

Once I'm cuffed, the officer takes my wrists in hand and pulls me out of the office and down the hallway until we're outside. I'm so relieved to be away from the loud alarm that I sigh with relief.

He stops at a squad car, and I see several other police vehicles make their way up Dad's long driveway. I keep expecting this guy to ask me who I am and what I'm doing at the house, but other than "Freeze" and "Put your hands up," there's been nothing.

Several car doors open, then slam shut. Footsteps approach from behind me. "Name?" someone to my left asks.

I answer before I even see a face. "Daisy Buchanan."

Then I hear "Daisy, what the fuck?"

Turning, I see Gage stomping up the driveway like he's marching into war.

By the time he's in front of me, I have a smile on my face. "Hi, Gage."

"Don't," he snaps. "What the fuck are you doing here?" He points at the house.

"That's my dad's house. I came to get my stuff."

"You broke in?"

I shake my head at that. "No. I've got a key. I just didn't know the code for the alarm."

"The security company's on their way. They'll turn it off." He turns to face the guy with the gun. "Take off the cuffs."

"No way," the guy mutters. "She broke in."

"You heard her. She has a key." I'm staring up at him, and I've got to say, he looks angrier than... well, than anyone I've ever seen. His face is bright red, his brow is furrowed, and his lips are so thin the word hairlike jumps into my head. And his eyes. Geez. His eyes are squinty and twitchy. Not a good look for the usually handsome Gage.

"Sir," the young officer grumbles. I guess seeing that expression on Gage's face is enough for the guy. "Fine," he says with a huff.

As soon as he's removed the zip tie, I rub my wrists. That's also the moment I see another car pull up the driveway. Great. It's my dad. So much for getting my stuff and getting out of here.

"Uh, Gage?" I lean in and speak in a low voice.

"What?" he says, still sounding pissed.

"You need to go into my dad's office."

He still looks angry but not as much. "Why?"

"Big pink envelope."

"Huh?"

"There's a big pink envelope in his desk drawer."

"You touch it?"

Oh crap. "Yes."

"Goddamn it, Daisy." Gage runs his fingers through his hair. "Don't say a word about it right now. I've gotta make a call."

CHAPTER THIRTY-TWO

Gage

Now what? Daisy said she spotted a pink envelope in her father's desk, but I can't just enter his house without a warrant. And I can't see myself getting a warrant since I've got no reason to believe Dr. Buchanan was even in the building at the time of the murder.

Except....

I watch the good doctor step out of his top-of-the-line Mercedes. My eyes go directly to his coat. A trench coat. A *black* trench coat. My eyes skim down to his feet and spot a pair of shiny dress shoes.

To myself I whisper, "Now, if you only had a hat." There may be something inside his car if I could just get a peek inside. Without thinking, I march over to Dorian Buchanan's car. "Mr. Buchanan." I smile. "False alarm."

"If that's the case, why is my daughter standing next to a police car?"

"She said she used her key to get in, which set off the alarm."

"Uh-huh." His eyes are on Daisy. "May I speak to my daughter?"

"Sure." I smile again. "Head on over." *And while you do that, I'll look inside your vehicle.*

With his back to me, I turn and peer down into his car. I look at the front seat first, then step back to check out the back seat. There it is. The hat in Dorian Buchanan's back seat looks identical to the one in the video. A fedora like a man from the 1950s would wear. I guess it goes with the trench.

Reaching into my pocket, I grab my cell and step away from the other officers to call the captain. When he answers, I get right to the point. "We need a warrant. Fast."

I listen as the captain asks me to keep the professor from entering his own home. Then he says, "Give me fifteen minutes. I'll call you back."

Stepping over to Daisy and her father, I hear him say, "The only way you're getting your things back is if you're living here." He points at the door. "And by finishing what you've started." He pauses. "Maybe I should press charges."

"You wouldn't." Daisy sounds shocked.

"Try me."

She must see me approach, because her eyes meet mine and she frowns. "Officer Golden, you remember my *father*."

"Of course." I smile, but it's only for show. "Do we have an issue here?"

"My dad won't give me back my things unless I move home. Or else he's going to press charges."

"Well, now, that's not exactly...", Dorian Buchanan attempts to backtrack.

"So, you'd like her to move home or else you're pressing charges for entering her own home? The one you want her to move back into? That doesn't make sense. It sounds like you're *blackmailing* her." I emphasize the word because I want to see his reaction. It's better than I expected.

Dorian rears his head back. "Blackmail?" He scoffs. "I'm not blackmailing my own daughter. How gauche."

Gauche? That's a word I haven't heard in... well, ever. "I don't know about that, but it sounds like you're giving her no options." I look at Daisy, then back at her father. The resemblance is uncanny. The two of them have the same dark hair and fair skin, but it's their eyes that are really similar. They're both a steel gray color. "Are you going to press charges, Dr. Buchanan? Because if you are, you'll need to accompany me to the station to fill out the paperwork."

It's probably wrong, but I hope he presses charges. That'd give us ample time to obtain a search warrant.

With a sigh, Dorian Buchanan rubs a hand over his chin where a thin beard has begun to grow. Looking at his daughter, he says in a soft voice, "You need to move home, Daisy. For your own good."

"For my own good?" She scoffs. "That's rich. You think you know what's good for me?" She looks at me, smiling. "I've got a place to stay. Right, Gage?" She glares at her father. "I'm fine where I am."

I do my best not to smile at her statement. We don't need it getting around that she's staying with me. Not yet, anyway.

"What're you talking about?" His steely gaze hits me.

He knows. But he doesn't ask. Instead, he says, "I *do* know what's good for you, Daisy. Better than anyone else."

"Ha! That's a joke, *Dad*." Turning, Daisy starts to walk toward the house. "I'm getting my stuff."

"No you're not!" Dorian shouts and steps in front of her to block her path. "You're forbidden from entering that door until you agree that staying here is the right thing to do."

"No." She raises her arms and shoves her father's chest. "Fucking." She does it again, which forces Dorian to take a step back to catch his balance. "Way." She shoves him once again, and this time he can't stop the momentum. He lands on his ass on the pavement.

"Daisy," I say, approaching the pair. Placing my hand on her shoulder, I say softly, "Stop."

Dr. Buchanan pushes himself to the side, then up on his knees until he's standing. Pointing at his child, he shouts, "For *that*, I'm pressing charges."

"Dr—"

"She assaulted me, and I've got about six witnesses."

I look back at the other cops and the security company rep who just showed up. They're all watching the scene. He's right. He's got six very reliable eyewitnesses.

"Do you need me to call for an ambulance?" I mean, if he's hurt, he should be seen by first responders.

"I'll go to my personal doctor after I fill out the paperwork." He glares at Daisy.

Needing for Dorian to stay away from his own home, I give this a try. "Would you like to ride with me or—"

"No. I'll meet you at the police station." He turns to walk toward his car. Which is good except for the part where Daisy gets cuffed again.

"Gage?" she says, sounding frightened.

"I've got this. Just go with the patrol officer. I'll see you at the station." She blinks at me, and I'm afraid she's going to cry. So, stopping in front of her, I look into her eyes. "Do you trust me?"

She thinks for a moment. "Yes."

"Then go with the officer. I'll see you soon."

EVERYTHING WORKED BETTER THAN I COULD HAVE HOPED. I followed Dr. Buchanan's vehicle all the way to the police station, where he now sits in an interview room. I was able to convince him not to go back into his home until the security company and an officer had a chance to make sure everything was okay. What I actually did, though, was ask the officer to stand watch and not allow anyone besides the security company in, and to make sure all they did was punch in the code and leave.

In the meantime, Captain Billings was able to secure a search warrant. While the search team heads to Dr. Buchanan's home, I get to be the one who tells him what's happening.

"Dr. Buchanan?" I say, stepping into the interview room.

"It's about damn time," he growls. "Why does it take so damn long to press charges?"

"Well." I pull out the chair across from him and sigh. "It looks like you'll be here a bit longer."

"No." He stands. "I've got things to do. Papers to grade."

All A's, I'd bet.

"Please take a seat, Dr. Buchanan."

He does so, albeit slowly.

"Unfortunately, I'll need you to stay until they're finished searching your home and vehicle."

"My home and... what?" he shouts. "What the hell?"

Placing the warrant down in front of him, I give him the abbreviated version. "As you can see by this court document, we're searching your home and vehicle for any articles or information related to the murder of Kara Becker."

"The what?" Dorian jumps out of his chair again, this time reaching across the table.

That's when Finch steps in and says, "Sit. Or I'll cuff you to the chair."

Buchanan sits. "What the hell's going on?"

Just then, my phone chimes with a message from Dan. I open it to see shots of the contents of the pink envelope. They look similar to the photos we found beneath Kara's mattress, except in these, you can see faces.

"Sir. Did you know the deceased, Kara Becker?"

"I.... She was a student of mine."

"Is that all?"

"Yes." He leans back, crossing his arms and taking on what I'd call defiant body language. "Of course that's all."

I turn my phone so he can see one of the images Dan just sent me. "Is this you, here?" I point at the image of a naked Dorian Buchanan.

He blinks several times, looks up at me, then back down at the image, and asks, "Where did you get that picture?"

"*We're* asking the questions," snaps Finch.

On my phone, I change the image. "Or how 'bout this one? Is this you?"

It's a shot of just his face, his head on a pillow next to Kara Becker.

"Look," he says, running a hand over his scruffy beard. "We... we were seeing each other. There's nothing wrong with it. She was an adult."

"When did you two start 'seeing' each other?"

Buchanan thinks about it for several minutes. "Last fall."

"Was Kara in your class at the time?"

He nods slowly.

I look over at Finch but say nothing, making sure my expression doesn't change.

"Where did you get those pictures?" Buchanan asks.

"I think you know."

"No." He shakes his head. "I've never seen those before in my life."

"They were discovered in your home office."

"In my—" He tries to stand again, but Finch has his hand on his shoulder before he can move. "I swear, I've never seen those pictures before in my life."

I switch the photo to the one of the envelope. "Have you seen this before?"

He blinks. Leans in closer. Blinks again. "I have."

"When?"

"When my students turn in their papers, I ask them to place them in individual envelopes."

I stay quiet, but he's not adding anything. "Who used bright, pink envelopes?"

"K—" He clears his throat. "Kara Becker used that type, I believe."

"Where were you on the night of Kara Becker's murder?"

"Home."

I nod at Finch, who steps into the booth, then returns with a laptop. Setting it down on the table, he turns it to face the doctor. "This shot from the elevator was taken the night of the murder at approximately 10:33 p.m. We have similar footage showing you leaving the premises the same way just over an hour later." Plenty of time.

Buchanan leans forward, watching as Finch hits Play. When he sees himself on-screen, he sits back abruptly. "I must've gone to see Daisy." He looks at the video, then back at me. "I did. I remember now. I went to see Daisy. She asked me to come."

I highly doubt that.

"We'll be sure to ask Miss Buchanan about *that*," Finch says, snapping the computer shut. Taking the laptop, he returns to the confines of the booth.

"We have you there, in the building, the night of the murder. We have images of you and Miss Becker in, well, in an amorous position. Images that could harm your reputation," I state.

"Kara and I stopped seeing each other. There was no reason for me to kill her."

"We have Miss Becker's journal. She mentions getting money from someone. Did she ask you for money in exchange for those images?"

"No. Of course not." He slaps his palm down onto the table. "There's nothing wrong with her and I—"

"Did her grade jump from an F to an A before or after you slept with her?"

His face blanches.

I've got him.

"She did the necessary work to improve her grade. Both semesters."

"Uh-huh."

"She did," he says angrily. "There's nothing in our contracts that says we cannot date students."

"Date?" I frown. "Did you two date? Were you courting?"

"Courting?" He scoffs. "I'm married."

"So 'affair' is a better word, isn't it? How would your wife feel about you sleeping with another woman?"

"How the hell would I know? She won't return my calls."

Daisy said something similar.

"The last I heard, she was in Utah or somewhere out in the boonies," he continues.

I think Daisy mentioned California. I stand, picking up my notebook. "I'll be right back." I want to give Buchanan enough time to stew on this conversation, plus I want to ask Daisy about her father's visit. She never mentioned that either.

In the booth, I stop in front of Finch and the captain.

"I think you've got him," Captain Billings says with a smile.

I think I do too. "I'm going to ask Daisy about his claim that he was there to see her."

"Good." He smiles. "I'll watch him squirm until you get back."

Out in the main room of Ames PD, I grab a set of keys and head back to the holding cells. I hate the idea that she's back here, locked up. When I reach her cell, she's lying on a cot, her eyes red and puffy.

"Honey," I say softly.

"Gage?" She jumps up from the cot and races to the bars. "Can I go now?"

"Not yet. I need to ask you something."

"Okay." Her voice is hesitant.

"We have footage of your father taking the elevator from the parking garage up to your floor the night of the murder."

Daisy gasps.

"He says he was there to see you. Is that true?"

"No." Her face looks fierce. "He's lying."

"He said you asked him to come."

Scoffing, she grabs the bars between us. "Like I'd call him."

"That's what I thought." Turning, I reach out and touch one of her hands. "I'll be back."

"Hurry, Gage." She sniffles. "I've always hated being locked up."

That's a strange way of putting it, but I get what she means. "I'll be back."

"Okay."

CHAPTER THIRTY-THREE

Gage

"We've got him at the scene at the time of the murder. We've got a motive—Kara's blackmail scheme," Captain Billings notes.

"He must be the dude who had 'bank,' according to Dylan Forrester."

"Agree," I say as I write down the captain's summary. "When we went back in to speak to him, to tell him Daisy denied his claim that she'd asked him to visit, he then claimed to have seen someone else in the hallway outside of Kara's apartment as he was leaving."

"Right," Finch grumbles. "We've identified every person who came and went from the front and back entrances of Becker's building. Besides residents, there's been no others who left around that time."

I shrug. "It could have been a resident. You know, walking by her door."

"He said the guy was *knocking* on her door."

The captain stands and paces in front of the small conference room. "Let's show the professor a picture lineup. Include all of the players and see if he picks someone we've already vetted."

Finch gets the task of creating the photo lineup. He's including Dylan Forrester, Luke Green, Bryant Falco, and seven others, some of whom came from Kara Becker's social media accounts. Once it's prepared, Finch is given the pleasure of placing the lineup in front of Dr. Buchanan while we watch from the booth.

"Please look at all ten photos and point to the person you believe you saw in the hallway outside of Kara Becker's apartment."

We watch as Dorian scoots his chair closer to the table. He leans down over the pictures. His head moves from my right to left and back again.

"Doubt he points to anyone," mumbles the captain.

I'm not so sure. He's gone back to the same part of the page several times. When he raises his hand, first finger extended, I hold my breath. Almost in slow motion, Buchanan moves his finger down, pressing on one image. "*That* one."

"That one?" Finch asks, looking perplexed.

"Yeah. He was outside her door. Knocking."

Finch says aloud, "Let the recording show that Dr. Dorian Buchanan picked number seven from the photo lineup."

I look down at the photocopy and blink. Buchanan just fingered, Bryant Falco. *What the ever-loving hell?*

Finch steps back into the booth looking perplexed. "I questioned his roommates; they all corroborated his story. He was back home that night."

"He could still have made the drive back, the little bastard," the captain growls. "It's forty minutes tops from his parents' home to Kara's."

"Buchanan could be lying." Finch makes a good point.

Captain Billings stands up, handing Finch his copy of the lineup. "I'm starting to think *everyone*'s lying."

He's not the only one.

"Go on in there, Golden. Follow up with his claim that he was there to visit Daisy."

"Yeah." I nod. "Okay."

FINCH STAYS IN THE BOOTH JUST AS DAN RETURNS FROM Buchanan's house after sending the pink envelope off to be fingerprinted. Meanwhile, I step into the interrogation room to speak with Dorian. "I talked to Daisy."

Not only that, but we've had a chance to search his car since it was parked right outside our door. There, we got the hat and his cell. Luckily the district attorney made sure to include his cell phone in the search; otherwise, we wouldn't have been able to download his text messages to the deceased. We also downloaded messages between Dorian and Daisy from the day of the murder. There were none from her asking Dorian to stop by the building. Call records do show the two spoke that day for less than two minutes. She could have asked him to stop by, but there's no way of knowing. I'll need to ask her about that exchange after I speak with Dorian.

"And?" Dorian's acting quite cocky considering he's been cooped up in this little room in the police station for the last couple of hours.

"She denies your claim that she asked you to visit."

"She would."

"What do you mean?"

Ignoring my question, he has one of his own. "So, she's living with you now?"

I quickly look at the two-way glass, but I choose not to respond. "What did you mean by 'she would'?"

"You know." He sighs, leaning back in his chair. Crossing one leg over the other, he says, "I'm not sure you're the person I should be speaking to. As a matter of fact, I'd like my attorney."

"You haven't been Mirandized—"

"Then let me talk to the person in charge," he sneers. "After you let me call my attorney."

I'm losing patience with this man. "If you're innocent, why wouldn't you just answer my questions?"

"Says the man living with my daughter."

I hear the door open and already know who's entered.

"Dr. Buchanan." Captain Billings holds out his hand. "It's nice to meet you."

Okay. He's the good cop. I'm the fucking stupid one.

"Golden, will you please go ask Detective Turnbull to join me?" the captain says.

"Yep."

As I stand to leave, Dorian says, "Hey."

I turn to face him. "What?" I want to wring this guy's neck, but I do my best to stay calm.

"I'm just curious." He scratches his chin. "*Which* Daisy have you been living with?"

"Excuse me?" What the fuck does that mean?

Then the asshole laughs.

I turn and am out of the room so fast, it'd make your head spin.

When I see Dan, he's scowling.

"You too?" I snap.

"You're living with the eyewitness?"

"She's staying with me." I run my fingers through my hair. "She had nowhere else to go."

Standing, Dan moves past me, stopping when we're only a foot apart. "Better not be screwing her."

"Eat shit, Dan."

"Jesus," he mumbles. "You're fucked, man."

I know.

I should leave, but I need to watch the rest of this show.

Pulling up a stool as Dan joins Billings in the interrogation room, I sit close to the two-way glass.

"You gonna do anything about that cop and my daughter?" Buchanan asks my boss.

"I don't know what you're referring to," the captain says diplomatically. Covering his own ass, no doubt.

"My daughter insinuated earlier that she's staying with that cop."

"I'll check into that." Billings sits back in his seat. "So, what did Daisy want?"

"Want?"

Impertinent asshole.

"Want. The night of the murder. You said she asked you to stop by. What did she want?"

He scoffs. "The same shit she always wants."

"Which is?"

"You know," Buchanan sighs like he's bored. "I really want a lawyer."

"We're making the call as we speak." The captain reassures. "What does Daisy usually need when she calls you?"

Buchanan sighs and rests his head back on his shoulders. Raising it again, he looks directly at the captain. "She's got issues."

"Issues?" Dan asks.

"Problems."

The captain takes this one. "Problems?"

"She...." He leans forward and whispers, "Mental problems."

Fucking lies.

"It's why I pay all her bills, take care of her," he continues. "It's also the reason her mother left. She couldn't take it anymore."

What kind of father spews shit like this about his child?

"I'm sorry." The captain leans closer. "Can you be more specific?"

Buchanan sits up suddenly. "Not without my lawyer present."

"Very well," Billings says resignedly. Dan stands first, then the captain. "We'll let you know when he gets here."

"Great."

God, Dorian Buchanan is a smug bastard.

The minute the two are through the door of the booth, it slams shut and the captain yells, "My office. Now!"

Yeah. I'm screwed.

CHAPTER THIRTY-FOUR

Daisy

It's been hours and I'm still in a jail cell. And it's all my goddamn father's fault.

God, I *hate* him.

Everything is all his fault. *Everything.*

I was so close to having everything exactly how I wanted it, but then he did what he always does and fucked it up.

"Ahhhhh!" I scream as loud as I can from my cell. "Let me out of here!"

I hear the pounding of footsteps and smile inwardly. It's working.

"What's wrong?" asks a young cop I've never seen before.

Doing my best to get the waterworks going, I sob, "I c-can't be in here. I'm s-scared of small spaces."

"You're claustrophobic?" asks the other cop who joined him. A much older one.

"I am. I've always been a-afraid." I sniffle and cover my eyes. It's true, though. Ever since my pathetic excuse for a father had me locked up in the loony bin at age eight, where they housed me in a room that was, at most, five-by-five feet. I had a tiny cot and that was it.

"Can't I wait out there?" I point in the direction they just came from. "I'll apologize to my father. I was just upset. I didn't mean to push him."

"Miss...," the older cop starts.

I think of something sad—you know, like me not being free—and the tears really start to fall. "I can't be in here."

With the voice of a man who actually cares about other people, the older man says, "Give me a minute, sweetheart. Let me see where we're at on all of this."

As the pair walk away, I can hear them. They're arguing. The young guy thinks I should stay put, but the old one is 100 percent team Daisy.

It's too bad fucking Gage isn't. Where the hell is he, anyway? It's been hours since he asked me if I had my father stop by my place that night.

God. This is all such a joke.

CHAPTER THIRTY-FIVE

Gage

This probably won't shock you, but I'm off the case. Not only am I off the case, but I'm on paid administrative leave as well. The captain told me to take a couple of weeks to "think about my priorities." I'm not sure what he means.

Actually, yes I do.

He wants me to spend time pondering whether or not I want to be a cop.

It's a good question. I mean, I *thought* I wanted to be a cop. I don't remember a time in my life when I didn't want to be an officer of the law. But now?

I'm not so sure.

To make matters worse, I wasn't allowed to go back in to see Daisy, to explain why I was no longer able to help her with her father's charge against her. Hell, even with him being questioned for the murder of Kara Becker, he still declined to drop it.

So now I'm home. I've changed into sweats, a tee, and a hoodie with the intention of going for a run, but I can't seem to leave my house.

What if Daisy gets released?

She doesn't have a key to my place. Not yet, anyway.

204 · KAYT MILLER

"Fuck."

Pulling my phone out of my hoodie pocket, I shoot off a quick text. Then, before I can talk myself out of it, I grab my keys and wallet and slip them in the front pocket along with my phone, and head out, leaving the front door unlocked in case Daisy returns. A run will clear my head, and there's nothing I need more than that right now.

My usual route is about five miles, but I've got another one, a longer one, that I decide to take today. Turning left in front of my house instead of right, I jog down to Lincolnway, which is one of the main thoroughfares in Ames. From there, I head west past some of the dormitories and Welch Avenue. I'm tempted to stop at Cy's to... what, talk to Luke? Have a beer? But, I don't. Instead of turning onto Welch Avenue, I continue west.

By the time I've jogged to the large grocery store in west Ames, I know I've reached the halfway point. With my hands on my waist, I bend to take in some air. So far, all this run has done was wind me. My head's still full of... well, full of thoughts I can't seem to organize.

"Gage?"

Hearing my name makes me jump a little. It's unexpected. Pulling myself up to stand, I look left.

"Over here."

To my right, I see someone familiar. "Oh, hey, Kat."

Stepping over to me, she smiles. "What're you doing?"

I point to my attire. "Out for a run." I look at her clothing. She's got on a sweatshirt and exercise pants along with a cool pair of running shoes. "What about you?"

"Also out for a run." She laughs. "The Beedle Babes have been taking morning walks for a while now, and it's been good, but I decided to up my game and added a run to my routine twice a week. I'm working up to doing a 5K next spring."

"Good for you." I smile. "I've done a couple of those."

"And would recommend them?"

"Sure. It's a great goal." I can't think of anything else to say.

"Are you heading east or west?" she asks, pointing east.

"East. Heading back to my place."

"Mind if I jog with you for a bit?" She blushes. "I'm sure you'll want to pull away after a block, but we could start out together."

Not really. I'd prefer to run alone, but I'm not going to be rude. "Sure."

We start off at a slow pace, which is okay with me. I'm tired from, well, everything. My sleep schedule is off too, which isn't helping.

"So, how's the investigation going?" Kat asks.

I'm not sure why I say it, maybe because I'm tired, but I blurt, "I'm off the case."

She stops running suddenly, "What? Why?"

"I started seeing the eyewitness."

Kat's blinking at me. Her face morphs from something pretty to something angry. Jamming her hands on her hips, she spits, "You're sleeping with the person who told you that Tayler murdered Kara?"

"That's not what she told me."

"Let me rephrase that." She glares at me., "So, you're sleeping with the person who claims Tayler was at the murder scene."

"Look, we've all but cleared Tayler, okay?" I sigh. "I started seeing her after I was sure Tayler was innocent."

"Oh." Her arms drop to her side. "Sorry."

"I get it. You're looking out for your friend. I'd do the same." Hell, I *was* doing the same.

"So, is that why you're off the case?"

I point to the east and start my jog again. Kat follows suit.

"Yes. My boss, the captain, told me to end things with her, but I—"

"Do you love her?"

My breath catches at her question. "Love?"

"Yeah. Do you love her? You must. You were taken off the case. You weren't willing to give her up. You must love her."

I can't say that. Not yet. "We've only just met."

Kat's breathing has become labored, but she keeps right on talking. "So you couldn't wait to date until after the investigation was over?"

I'm quiet for a block or two. Her question is a good one. *Why didn't I wait?* "I told her I wanted to wait, but I guess I... I don't know. I should have waited." It would have been best for Daisy in the long run. I could be helping her get out of jail right now rather than running away from my problems—literally.

"Maybe it's not too late. Maybe talk to your boss about it. Tell him you were smitten and you didn't think it through."

That's not going to work.

"Oh, I know." Kat reaches out and takes hold of my arm. I slow down to a walk. "Just tell him you'll wait. That your job is your priority right now. I mean, if it's meant to be with this girl, it will be."

Stopping again, I look at Kat. "Do you really feel that way?" It sounds like a rather fanciful notion, if you ask me.

"Of course." She shrugs. "I believe in fate. Why wouldn't I?"

"Fate?"

"Yeah. Like us running into each other." She slaps my arm and giggles. "Get it. Run into each other?"

I smile at her. She's always been so quiet whenever I've been around the ladies from Beedle Drive, but I guess I'm usually investigating something when I see them. I'd be quiet too. "I get it."

"Hey, let's grab a beer." I look up and see we've stopped on the corner of Welch and Lincolnway.

I glance to my right and wonder if Daisy's home yet. Even if she is, do I want to see her?

That's not the right question. No, the question is will *she* want to see *me*?

"Sure," I reply after a moment.

"We could eat too," Kat says, starting up the hill toward the bar. "Fried pickles, here I come."

"Do you think that's the way to go if you're training for a 5k?"

"Sure. Why not?" She smirks at me. "I'll burn off about five pickles on the way back."

"Sounds about right." I laugh as I catch up and walk next to her. "What about a burger and fries? Think I can burn those off in a few miles?"

"Sure." Kat grasps the handle to Cy's and opens the door. "My guess, you'd burn off eight fries and one bite of cheeseburger in three miles."

Reaching up, I grasp the edge of the door and hold it open for her to enter. "Bet you're right."

"Of course I'm always right." Kat releases a little snort, and it makes me smile again. "As long as you remember that, we'll be fine."

I chuckle. "Have you had issues with this in the past? You know, people not knowing you're right all the time?"

Finding a table in the back, Kat slides into a booth and nods. "It's why my two-year relationship ended."

"Oh, I'm sorry."

She shrugs. "Well, that and he cheated on me."

"Shit."

Waving it away, she smiles. "It's fine." She shakes her head. "Not really, but that was a couple of months ago. I'm really fine. Now that I'm on the other side of it, I'm glad it happened. He... well, he wasn't the man I thought he was, and I learned he wasn't the kind of man I want to end up with. I want an honest, stand-up guy."

I'm tempted to ask her what she means by that, but a waitress approaches to ask us what we'd like to order. We both select a beer on tap along with fried pickles, a cheeseburger each, and a basket of fries. Once the waitress leaves, it's quiet for the first time since we ran into each other.

"So, you're okay now?" I ask softly.

"Single and ready to mingle," Kat says with a smile. Then she adds, "Just kidding. No, I feel good. It was difficult, sure, but for the best. I really mean that."

"That's good."

She reaches out and taps the top of my hand with one of her fingers. "I know there's more, Gage, so spill. Tell me everything that's going on with you."

My eyes find hers, and I know for certain she's sincere. She cares. The question is, can I trust her?

She must be a mind reader, because she holds up three fingers and says, "I won't tell a soul. Scout's honor."

"You were a scout?"

"Sure. I was a Girl Scout, a Brownie, *and* a Bluebird."

"Wow. Okay. Consider yourself vetted."

"Awesome."

So I talk. I tell her everything—well, not anything related to the case, but everything from the moment I saw Daisy's eye in the small opening in her door to today and the events that landed her in jail. I think I've shocked her with the last part.

"She's in jail? Right now?" She points down at the table.

"I believe so, yes."

"And you can't help her?"

Our food arrives, and we go quiet as we open our utensils and prepare to eat.

"Not right now, no," I finally reply. "One of the guys I was working with, Lance Finch, said he'd do what he could." And for some fucking reason, I believe him. "She's going to be upset." I don't think Daisy is going to understand that I was in no position to barter for her release. As angry as the captain was, anything I tried would have probably made things worse for her. I shrug. "Maybe it's a sign."

"Oh, so now *you're* all about fate?" Kat smirks as she bites into a fried pickle dipped in ranch dressing. "You want to know what I think?"

"Sure." Why not?

"I think she'd be crazy not to understand the situation you're in."

I'm listening. "You think?"

"I do."

"Why?"

"Because, Gage, you're what we single women call a unicorn."

I put my hand on the top of my head.

Nope. No horn.

"A what?" Then I laugh. "What the hell does that mean?"

Taking a drink from her beer, Kat explains. "A unicorn is a guy who's the whole package. A unicorn is kind, sexy, smart, and loyal. They love their woman with everything they've got. They're protective, but not in a bad way. They're rare. Like the unicorn."

"Unicorns don't exist." And neither do guys like Kat's describing.

"They do, but like I said, they're very rare. And you're one of them."

"I'm not." Really, I'm not. I left Daisy alone in a damn cell, for shit's sake.

"Just take a compliment, will ya?" She laughs.

"I can take a compliment, but that's putting a lot of pressure on me."

"Nah." She shakes her head. "You can't help it. It's who you are."

I have no idea where she got these ideas about me, but I'm no goddamn unicorn.

I drink the last of my beer and set the glass down just as my phone chimes. Looking down at the screen, I see it's Finch. He's finally getting back to me after I sent him a text before my run. Holding up my finger, I tell Kat I've got to take the call. Sliding out of the booth, I walk to the back of the bar where it's a little quieter.

"Golden," I answer quickly.

"Man, you won't believe the shit that just went down here."

"What?" *Please don't tell me Daisy's hurt.*

"We just got the fingerprints back from the pink envelope and the photos."

Here we go. "And?"

"The outside of the envelope had Daisy's prints like we expected. It also had Kara's and Dorian Buchanan's."

"We expected that as well. So what's the issue?"

"It's the photos on the inside."

"Yeah?" *Jesus. Spit it out, man.*

"They only had one set of prints on them."

I hold my breath, waiting. "Whose prints?"

CHAPTER THIRTY-SIX

Gage

"Thanks for coming," the captain says with a scowl. "As soon as we've got this wrapped up, you and me, we're gonna sit down and talk about all of this. Yeah?"

I nod, but I'm not actually listening to him. Instead, I'm looking through the two-way glass into the interrogation room at Dan, who's sitting across from someone I care about. "So you think *Dan* should be the one to talk to her?"

"I do. You're too close to her."

"Don't you think she needs a lawyer?"

"Finch Mirandized her. She waived her right to an attorney."

Damn it, Daisy. I see my scowl in the reflection on the glass.

I should be in there with her.

"Dan's able to ask the tough questions without it being personal."

Now my reflection reads irritation. *I'm* able to separate my personal feelings... well, shit, maybe he's right.

"Let's see if Dan can find out what happened that night." He shrugs. "Hell, maybe we're wrong about everything."

We both watch as Dan begins. "Daisy, my name is Detective Trumbull. I'd like to ask you a few questions."

"Where's Gage?" she asks. "You told me Gage was going to be here."

"He's on his way." Dan pretends to jot something on a piece of paper. "The sooner we get done here, the sooner you can talk to Gage."

That's bullshit. I hate that he's lying to her.

"So let's get started, okay?"

"Okay." Daisy smiles sweetly.

"Let's talk about the pink envelope."

In milliseconds, her smile falls and a frown appears. "The one in my father's desk?"

"That one, yes."

"What about it?"

"How did the pink envelope end up in his desk?" Dan asks.

"I put it there."

I can't believe she just admitted to that.

"When?"

"Today. I took it into the house with me and put it there. *Duh*."

I guess it was as simple as that.

"There were photos inside," Dan tells her, though of course she already knows.

She sits quietly.

"Photos of your dad and Kara."

Still no reaction from her until Dan says, "They were having an affair."

"I know." Her voice is firm and unwavering.

"How did you know?"

"I followed them."

She what?

"Why did you follow them?"

With a shrug, she sits back in her chair and crosses her legs. "I just needed to know what he was up to."

"Why did you need to know that?"

"Because. *He's* always monitoring *me*. It was my turn to do the same to him. I wanted to show him what that felt like."

"Did he know? That you were following him?"

With a shrug, she looks at her fingernails.

Dan keeps going. "Why did you take the photos, Daisy?" His voice has gotten soft, almost friendly. He's trying to put her at ease.

I'm afraid of what she'll say next.

Slapping her palm down onto the table suddenly, she growls, "Because. Why does he get to do whatever *he* wants? Cavorting with students." She pretends to shiver. "It's disgusting." Pointing at Dan, she adds, "He's still fucking married to my mother."

"I understand." He says it so quickly I'd be surprised if she understood a word out of his mouth.

"It's disgusting. Don't you think?"

"Sure." Dan nods.

I give her words some thought. Dorian's relationship with Kara is definitely inappropriate, but disgusting? I can't go that far.

I scoot my seat closer to the window. The urge to reach out and touch her is so strong I have to fight it.

"So, what did you plan to do with the photos?" Dan asks.

She shrugs. "I needed money."

"From your father?"

"No." She scoffs. "That penny pincher. Kara was going to pay me for them."

"Kara? Why would she pay for the photos?"

"Because." She rolls her eyes like Dan's an idiot. "I threatened to tell her father about her little affair and about her sudden grade improvement."

Daisy knew about Kara's grades?

Dan asks, "Did you help your dad with his grades?"

Wait. She told me she hadn't helped him.

"Of course." Another hard eye roll. "My father is a lazy asshole. Hell, I write his books and papers for him too."

Wait? What?

"Is that how you got the pink envelope? When you graded for him?"

"Yeah. Kara submitted her papers in it."

Which is how it has both Kara's and Dorian's fingerprints. But here's the part I wish Dan would ask her about. She writes for her father?

"You said Kara was going to pay you. Did she?"

"Some."

"But not all?"

Daisy's voice lowers, and she growls, "No."

"Why not?"

She looks off to her right.

"Why didn't she pay you, Daisy?"

"She said she didn't have the cash, but I knew she was lying. She'd just gone shopping. She came home with a whole new outfit. A pretty flowered dress, shoes, the works."

A flowered dress? She was wearing a flowered dress....

No.

"When was this?"

Daisy looks at Dan and then at me. Or at the two-way glass. Her eyes pierce my heart. "Is Gage here yet?"

Yes.

"Not yet." He shifts some of his papers around on the table. "Was it that night, Daisy?"

"I'm not sure. I don't remember."

"Daisy, I need you to be honest with me."

"Honest with you?" She slaps the table again. "What do you want me to say? You want me to tell you I killed her?" Her head jerks closer to Dan. "Huh?"

My body is frozen in place. I can barely breathe.

"Well, I did. That fucking bitch wouldn't pay me a cent. She said she didn't care if her father knew." With a scoff, she adds, "She didn't even want to see the new pictures."

New pictures? Was Dorian still seeing Kara?

Standing suddenly, Daisy jabs a finger at Dan. "I had plans for that money. I was going to get the hell out of Ames, start a new life without my fucking father breathing down my neck."

"Daisy—"

"No." Her body turns slightly as she takes a step.

I stand as well and place my hands on the glass. Her demeanor changed so suddenly, it made the hair on my arms stand on end. Without looking at him, I tell the captain, "She needs a lawyer." Or a psychologist. "Does her father know she waived her rights?"

"Yes."

I turn to look at Billings. "And he's letting this go on?" *What kind of father does that?*

The captain's voice is suddenly gentle. "He said he's been dealing with her for long enough."

I scoff. "So he's just giving her up?"

"She murdered someone, Gage."

It makes no difference. Dorian Buchanan should be doing whatever he can to protect his child, but he's not.

But neither am I.

My attention is drawn back to Daisy as Dan says, "Have a seat, Daisy." His voice dropped an octave with those words.

Ignoring him, she takes one step. "This is all *his* fault."

"Your father's?"

"Yes!" she screams, taking another step closer. "I should have fucking killed *him* with that stupid golf club! He's the one who deserves to die."

She's around the side of the table now.

"Daisy. Please sit."

Her voice suddenly changes from angry and loud to soft and sweet. "You believe me, right?" The sound coming from her is almost creepy. "It's all my daddy's fault."

Daddy? She went from spewing vitriol about her father one minute and smiling sweetly the next. I think I may understand why her father asked me which Daisy lived with me. I think there may be more than one.

"Daisy," Dan says softly. "Please sit. Let's talk."

Right then, Finch steps into the interrogation room. Hell, I didn't even know he was here. From my vantage point, I see him smile as he says, "Hey, Daisy."

"Oh." Her face falls. "It's you."

"Yep, it's me. The guy who loved your cookies."

Smart thing to say. I could tell Daisy was close to losing her cool.

That makes her smile. "I'm a good cook." She beams as she moves away from Dan.

"You are."

I'm not sure why, but at that moment, Dan makes a stupid mistake by announcing, "Daisy, I'm afraid we'll need to take you back to the holding cell."

"No!" The scream that comes out of her is best described as bloodcurdling. "Not you too."

She lunges for Dan, but before she can get to him, Finch has her on the ground. He slips on cuffs as Daisy writhes on the ground while shouting obscenities.

I should do something. I should help her, them. But all I seem to be able to do is stare at the scene in front of me.

How did I not see any of it? Was I so blind and desperate for someone to love that I wasn't able to see the murderous forest for the beautiful trees?

God, I'm a shit cop.

I STARE AS THEY ESCORT DAISY BACK TO THE HOLDING CELL. She's literally kicking and screaming, while I sit in the booth, frozen. I can't move. Hell, I can't even think.

"How could I have been so wrong?"

"It happens, son." The captain's voice sounds sort of soft. I don't like it.

"Not to me." I scoff. "I thought I was a good cop."

"You are. You're an excellent cop. You just let yourself fall for that girl. If what her father says is true, Daisy's had problems for a long, long time. It's why he didn't want her to have visitors and why he monitored her."

I want to believe that, but something tells me Dorian Gray Buchanan is just as culpable in all this as Daisy. "She needs a good lawyer."

"Her father said he had a call in."

"She needs help, sir." Not to be locked away in a prison cell for the rest of her life.

"She does, but she killed a young woman, and for that, she needs to pay."

I know. I just can't say it.

In a slightly upbeat tone, he adds, "The good news is they dropped the charges against Tayler."

"Good." I nod, but I don't feel excited about the news. I'm sure the women on Beedle Drive will all be thrilled it's over.

"Go home, son. Come in bright and early. We need to talk."

About whether or not I've got a job, no doubt.

Hell, do I even *want* the job? Maybe being a cop isn't for me.

But what else is there?

EPILOGUE

Six Months Later

I pause my work in the kitchen when a knock sounds on my front door. "It's open," I say loud enough for her to hear, then wait and watch.

When she opens the door, a big smile slides across her face, which causes a chain reaction. Like my heart jumping in my chest at the sight of her. I smile back, of course. When she walks around the counter, gets up on her tiptoes, and kisses me on the cheek, saying, "Hey, babe," I feel it everywhere.

Turning to face her, I lean down and kiss her lips. "Hey. How you doin'?"

"Good now, unicorn."

I roll my eyes. She doesn't call me "unicorn" often, but every once in a while, she throws it out there. "I'm just an average man, Kat."

"Ha! You're definitely *not* average, Gage." She laughs, then pats my ass as she moves around me to the fridge. "Beer?"

I'm not sure if she's asking me if she can have one or if I want one. The answer to both is "Yes."

"Ooh, you got the good stuff." She sets a couple bottles of a local brew next to the steaks on the counter, and I reach out to open hers. Those caps can be tough.

"See?" She points at the bottle. "Right there. You didn't even think about it. You just took my bottle to open it because you know I have a hard time getting the caps off."

"And?" I hand her back an open bottle.

"That's unicorn shit."

I laugh as I tap my bottle against hers. "Just a man, Kat."

With an eye roll, she leans a hip on my counter. "What can I do to help?"

"Make the salad?"

Tonight we're celebrating, sort of. This will be our first party since we've decided to be official. It took a long time to get to this point, something I insisted on after everything with Daisy.

Daisy.

Whenever I think of her, my heart hurts. And not because I feel sorry for myself. No, I feel sorry for *her*. Mind you, I'm not happy she played me like she did, like a fucking piano, but she was —*is*—mentally ill. That's not my diagnosis, it was the court ordered psychiatrist's. Because of that, she never did stand trial. Her lawyer was able to use insanity as a defense, and the Story County District Attorney's office made a deal. She's in a maximum-security mental health facility in Northwest Iowa now and will be for many years.

The day after Daisy confessed to killing Kara, she and her attorney sat down with Finch and me in the interrogation room. I guess her lawyer advised her it'd be in her best interest to cooperate. She was subdued and exhausted. I could tell she'd spent the night crying by her red, puffy eyes, but the interesting part about it was how normal she seemed. The day before, she was erratic— smiling one minute, growling the next. But the day she confessed, she was the Daisy I recognized. And in the course of that conversation, she told us about her safety deposit box at First National Bank that held more photos of Kara and Dorian and a few of just

Dorian doing mundane things like grocery shopping and jogging. She also gave us the combination to a storage unit where she kept her other computer and the clothing she wore the night of the murder. In all, it was pretty cut and dry. I think she was almost relieved to have the truth out there.

Not everyone was happy with the outcome, however. Kara Becker's father for one. He's suing Dorian Buchanan for wrongful death. I suppose you're wondering how he could do that. Well, Becker feels that since Dorian knew Daisy's diagnosis, knew she was dangerous and still let her live across the hallway from his daughter unchecked, he should be liable.

So far, the case hasn't been thrown out, so we'll see if it'll hold water. I'm not so sure.

As for Dorian? He took a leave of absence from Iowa State University. I'm not sure if that was his idea or the university's, but I'd be surprised if he came back since they learned that most of his published work was done by Daisy. It's grounds for losing his tenure, and his reputation is in shambles.

"So, how was patrol last night?"

I'm brought back to the here and now by Kat's question. "Good. A little boring. Nothing major happened. Some speeding tickets, and a couple asshole students thought it'd be funny to knock down a few stop signs in Campustown."

I'm back on my regular patrol duties per my request. While I enjoyed many aspects of detective work, this is what I need right now. Perhaps in the future, I'll request the change, but not right now. No, right now I want to focus on other things. Like the person standing in my kitchen. The one who makes me smile every single day. The one who made sure *I* was okay after everything with Daisy happened.

"Idiots," she grumbles. "How drunk were they?"

I chuckle at her response. "They weren't."

"I repeat, idiots."

"Yep."

We smile at each other. And we look. I start at her dark hair. It's down today and shiny, as usual. Her face looks fresh and makeup free, but I know she has some on; she's definitely got something pink on her pretty lips. I scan down to her simple V-neck tee above a pair of jeans with holes in the knees. Her feet are covered in a pair of Birkenstocks. They look like they've seen better days, but she must love them because she wears them every day. I like them too because they give me a chance to see what color her toenails are today. They're red.

"Cute toes," I say softly as they step closer to me.

"Everything about *you* is cute." Her voice has gotten soft and a little husky.

I recognize it. It's her sexy voice. I also know when I look into her eyes, they'll be dilated. We haven't done it yet. Sex. We've done a lot of other things, but not the actual deed, and that's on me. I hope to remedy that tonight after everyone leaves. I think we've done this right, because I wanted to take this thing with Kat and me slow. It's probably not fair to her, but after the speed with which I ended up in bed with Daisy and the rash decisions I made, I had to take things slow this time around.

The thing between Kat and me started while I was in Missouri. The captain insisted I take a couple weeks off after Daisy's confession, so I took the opportunity to head home to spend time with my family. While I was there, Kat and I talked almost every night. She started it off by getting my number from Quinn and calling me after hearing about Daisy. Her thoughtfulness touched me. She was concerned about me and my broken heart while I was only concerned about Daisy.

After I returned to Ames, Kat and I kept right on talking. For over a month we spoke almost every day. The days we didn't, I missed her. Then, sometime in the second month, we went for a run. She's stuck to her plan of doing a 5K this year, and I plan to do it with her. Watching her strive for her goals is one of my favorite things to do. Kat is intense when she's working toward a goal. She's like me in that way.

After that run, we met often for coffee, lunch, and dinner. We saw a couple of movies together. Then I made dinner for her one night at my house. That was the night I kissed her. I was nervous as hell because I wasn't sure she felt the same way about me. But the minute our lips touched, I heard her whisper, "Finally," and I knew.

I knew that this, Kat, was worth the wait.

THANKS FOR READING! IF YOU'D LIKE TO CHECK ANOTHER ONE of Kayt's books, here's a good one:

ISABELLE "IZZY" HARMON IS home again. Literally. After landing her first teaching gig, Izzy has found herself sleeping in her old room on an ancient twin bed that squeaks whenever she moves. Sure, she loves Honeywell, Iowa but part of her wanted to move to civilization rather than return to her old life after graduating from college. Farm life is in her blood but so is the man who lives next door. It's too bad he never saw her as more than his best friend's little sister.

It's true what they say... distance makes the heart grow fonder and four years away did nothing to quell the way Izzy's heart rate doubles whenever he's nearby. She hoped to get over it, but things don't always work out the way we hope.

Nashville "Nash" Watson never left. His goal of playing base-
ball in the majors flew out the window the second he found out
he was going to be a father. No regrets, though, because Nash
figured he'd return to Honeywell, Iowa to farm his family's land. It
was the only thing he knew for sure. Well, that and he's never
falling for another woman again. Ever.

Never say never, Nash.

ALSO BY KAYT MILLER

For more information: www.kaytmiller.com

Bedhead

Redhead

Deadhead

FarmBoy

Game Changer

One of a Kind

The Virginia Chronicles

Our of the Blue: The Flynns Book One

Mick'sology: The Flynns Book Two

Vested Interest: The Flynns Book Three

The Importance of Being Ernie: The Flynns Book Four

The Importance of Being Kennedy's: The Flynns Book Five

Quirky Girl: The Flynns Book Six

The Art of the Game

Lainie: The Palmer Sisters Book 1

Agatha: The Palmer Sisters Book 2

Sadie: The Palmer Sisters Book 3

Cortland: The Palmer Sisters Book 4

Keely: The Palmer Sisters Book 5

Violet: The Palmer Sisters Book 6

Molly: The Palmer Sisters Book 7

The Portrait Painter

Hopeful Romantic (Coming soon.)

Thanks to Margie Dill (Coming soon.)

ACKNOWLEDGMENTS

Thank you to everyone from Hot Tree Editing for editing this book from start to finish.

And an extra special thank you to Becky Johnson at Hot Tree Promotions for your advice, expertise, and positivity.

And to my beta readers. Your feedback and patience is essential to this process. Thank you!

And to my mom who is the wind beneath my wings. Literally.

ABOUT THE AUTHOR

Kayt grew up in the midwest surrounded by a loving family which included three brothers, one sister, and parents who always fostered her creative side.

Kayt wrote her first book when she couldn't find a story about a certain type of a woman and a specific kind of man. She called it *Game Changer* and it couldn't have been a more appropriate title. It changed her life in many ways.

Her goal, as a writer, is to write stories that relate to all of us, to make readers laugh and maybe cry sometimes. Kayt hopes her readers can escape into a fantasy, one that's actually possible. Sure, some of the stories are dubbed "Insta-love" but that's okay. She fell in love with her husband pretty damn fast and with her daughter the second she saw her. So, it's a thing, she swears.

facebook.com/authorkaytmiller

twitter.com/kaytmiller1

instagram.com/kaytmiller1

bookbub.com/profile/kayt-miller

THANK YOU!

It's because of you I get live in a dream world of book boyfriends and endless possibilities. Thank you for reading! I sincerely hope you like it.

And if you did, please leave a review.

If you'd like information on upcoming books and events, sign up for my newsletter here: www.kaytmiller.com

SNEAK PEEK: SEXY SAVIOR (RELEASING DECEMBER 6, 2020)

A Cocky Hero Club Book

Chapter 1: Ben

"Schilling. What the fuck happened to your face?" asks my boss Graham Morgan—in front of a roomful of my colleagues—just as I'm ready to begin a presentation I've been working on for weeks. A presentation that's sure to lead to a promotion.

Damn it. I thought I'd done a pretty good job minimizing the damage. I iced it as soon as I got back into the office and caught a glimpse of the swelling. Hell, it was already turning purple by that time. And since I lost one of my contact lenses during the... well, the ordeal, I had to dig out my old glasses—old glasses that one of my former girlfriends laughed at and dubbed "nerd glasses." Honestly, they are pretty nerdy with their thick black frames, but I figured they were big enough to disguise my injury.

Apparently not.

With a heavy sigh, I turn to Graham and attempt a smile, but it hurts like hell, so I wince instead. "Had a little accident over lunch break."

Graham chuckles. I guess I should be pleased he's laughing

about this, because if the same thing happened a month ago, before he met his girl, he'd have kicked my ass, metaphorically speaking. "You got punched in the face at lunch?"

I smile, or try to, pretending to find his line of questioning amusing because even though Graham is in a much better mood since meeting Soraya, he's still an asshole on a good day. "I wasn't punched." No, I was elbowed. Hard. "It was a misunderstanding."

Yeah, the misunderstanding was on *her* part. I mean, seriously, who elbows a guy in the face? Especially a guy who's trying to keep a woman from falling into oncoming traffic. Am I right?

"I figured you'd say, 'You should see the other guy.'"

I'm not sure who says that, and I don't really give two fucks. I just want this conversation to end.

"What happened? One of your heroic moments take a bad turn?"

I whip my head left in time to see my assistant nudge the guy next to him. He knows the backstory here. He knows about my little hobby—the one that was thrust upon me one rainy day. I never meant to be a superhero. It just happened.

But I can't get into that right now. Instead, I glare because... *fucking traitor*. I hate my assistant. He's a suck-up and an asshole. I swear he wants my job.

"No." I glare at Clive. Yeah, that's what I said. His name is *Clive*. "It was a misunderstanding."

"Go on." Graham waves his hand like he's shooing away a pesky rodent. "You might as well tell us the whole story. We're never going to be able to pay attention to your presentation until we know what really happened."

I stare at my boss, and the only thing I can tell you for sure is my fight-or-flight instinct is firmly in the flight category. But I can't run away. So, I do what I always do whenever shit isn't going my way—I smile.

"Sure." I fake chuckle. "I was heading out to lunch."

"We know," someone from the back of the fucking peanut gallery deadpans.

Ignoring that, I continue. "I was at the light ready to cross over 42nd when I happened to see someone with their shoe caught in a grate."

"Someone? Or a woman?" Peanut gallery again. The fuckers.

"A woman." And not just any woman. This one, well, let's just say she had my attention long before her shoe got stuck. No, I noticed her a couple blocks back, probably due to the tight red pencil skirt she had on. I've no idea about anything else, just her gorgeous ass and curves in that skirt. Oh, and the heels. Spiky stilettos. The kind that makes a man pause and picture those wrapped around him. Well, not the shoes, the legs attached to said shoes. Her heels were black and shiny and were connected to gorgeous, curvy legs. There was a line that ran down the back like a forties film star. *That's* why I noticed.

"She wasn't able to pull herself free, so I stepped over to her, reached down, and, well, I tried to help her."

She didn't like it. Not one bit. I guess I shouldn't have grabbed her leg. Maybe I should have reached for her foot instead. But I wasn't thinking. My first instinct was to help her—to save her from certain death. Sue me.

I snort and it's loud. She wouldn't have died. I'd never have let that happen. "When I tried to pull her foot free, she got startled."

That's a lie. She wasn't startled. She was pissed.

"She reacted, and her elbow came back and got me right in the eye."

Twice.

"Why are you limping?"

Fucking Clive.

"When her foot got free, it came down on top of mine."

Another lie. It wasn't an accident. She stomped down so hard, I wanted to cry on the spot, but I held it together. I guess I should be happy she didn't aim for my nuts.

"Who is this girl?" Graham asks, looking like he wants to hire her. I guess he could always use a good security guard, because that woman is lethal.

"I don't know." I barely saw her face. But what I did see was beautiful.

Her dark hair was all messy, falling around her face, probably from the struggle to free the shoe. The whole thing took only a couple of minutes before she was off, stomping across the street at a fast clip. Part of me was relieved she was gone while another wondered if I'll ever see her again.

For more information on > The Cocky Hero Club.